Baby in the Night is a gently surreal journey into and through the moonlit mind of Tony Volcano Ventura, who knows all the right questions but does not yet have the words to ask them. What a pleasure to read Kevin Sampsell's beautiful, loving, hilarious, endlessly surprising prose, and to see this realm through Tony's wise, astonished eyes. I loved crawling along with Tony between daytime world and nighttime world, seeing and believing, suspecting and knowing, secret poetry and slobbery dialogue. I adored *Baby in the Night* and I bet you will too. A sui generis marvel!

—KAREN RUSSELL, author of *The Antidote*

I didn't know I wanted to read a book narrated by a baby until I picked up *Baby in the Night* and was fully spellbound by its singular voice and view. This novel is one of those miracle books—it shouldn't work! But Sampsell shows us a whole suffering, precious world in a few small city blocks, as seen by one small person. A dreamlike pleasure from beginning to end.

—LYDIA KIESLING, author of *Mobility*

Kevin Sampsell has written a wholly unique novel from inside a child's mind, where reality and fable beautifully blur. Tony Volcano Ventura sneaks out of his big-boy bed to wander the nighttime streets, building meaning from fragments the way children do—through magical thinking, misheard words, and fierce, illogical love. *Baby in the Night* is a book about absence that somehow feels full, about a boy constructing a mythology to survive the unbearable wait for someone to come home. Sampsell's sentences are precise and deceptively simple, each one glowing from within.

—KIMBERLY KING PARSONS, author of *We Were the Universe*

In Sampsell's characteristically strange, raw, and tender style, we experience the world through the eyes-wide-open observations of the wondrous Tony Volcano—tiny baby, prodigy of the streets, human relationships, and the moon. It's really fucking good.

> —CHARLIE J. STEPHENS, author of *A Wounded Deer Leaps Highest*

Baby in the Night is a triumph of surreal weirdness and wonder. Kevin Sampsell is hands down the funniest writer I know; he also happens to have a heart the size of the moon.

> —JUSTIN HOCKING, author of *A Field Guide to the Subterranean*

In the exquisite *Baby in the Night*, Kevin Sampsell writes a coming-of-age story that isn't set in the typical adolescent pivot into adulthood but in early childhood when the world and human behavior have a sort of sci-fi oddness, beauty, and menace. A coming-of-being story. Our young hero Tony is on a quest to find out about his father. He watches and imbibes sensations, attentively noting the words and actions around him; permeable and inquisitive, finding the edges of things and people. There's a central mystery, a loss, like there always is in any life, and the answer will set the stage for the life to come. It's the most engrossing, tender, and quietly strange book I've read in ages.

> —NATE LIPPENS, author of *Ripcord*

Baby in the Night is whimsically surreal and wholly devastating. I'm not even quite sure I can describe all the things it made me feel. Contemplative, heartbroken, at times worried and delighted. Through young Tony's eyes, Sampsell asks us to consider what kind of world we'll be handing to the children who have yet to come.

> —ELLE NASH, author of *Deliver Me*

Baby in the Night is deliciously strange and delightfully surreal. Sampsell has once again written a book that will forever live in my head and my heart.
　　—CARLA CRUJIDO, author of *The Strange Beautiful*

Wowsers! Kevin Sampsell has written something so special with *Baby in the Night*. Tony Volcano, our toddler narrator, spoke directly to the child in me. He offered me his hand and led me through streets filled with violence and compassion. Tony Volcano is proof that sometimes the wisest person in the room might be the two-year-old. This book is surreal, funny, astute, biting, and always deeply moving, true magic. I'm not sure how Sampsell accomplished this feat of a novel, but I do know I'll be coming back to it for years to come, trying to figure out how he pulled it off.
　　—EMME LUND, author of *The Boy With a Bird in His Chest*

Reading *Baby in the Night* I entered a slightly fevered state of literary delirium. Absorbed and in awe of the novel's tender-hearted magic, I dropped all preconceived notions about how the world works and who I'd want to steer me through it. Baby in the Night was a welcome reminder that deep wells of endless wisdom live inside every single one of us, no matter our age. As always Kevin Sampsell amazed me with each line of prose, how spare and perfect and charged with meaning. Assign his sentences to any creative writing class and let writers be blessed with abundance. This is how you do it, folks. Word by word. Line by line. Until you've got *Baby in the Night*. Incredible.
　　—GENEVIEVE HUDSON, author of *Boys of Alabama*

Baby in the Night is *Harold and the Purple Crayon* for the defamiliarization set. Outstanding!
　　—CAREN BEILIN, author of *Sea, Poison*

I've been a fan of Sampsell's for years, and this new novel is beautiful lunacy. If this is a bedtime story, it's the most batshit one I've ever read.

—JOSHUA MOHR, author of *The Wolf Wants Answers*

Baby in the Night is surreal, tender and magnetic. Sampsell renders the slow-drip arrival of language in our baby-protagonist's mind with revelatory precision. No book better communicates how the language we use shapes the world we live in, and how we feel and see.

—RITA BULLWINKEL, author of *Headshot*

The most compelling part of Sampsell's book, which is written from the perspective of a street smart baby, is how it conveys the inarticulate instinct. Or how a thought or feeling can be perfectly clear on the inside, but emerge all scattered and snarled. *Baby in the Night* is a fairytale born out of abject poverty. With skewed and comic tenderness, Sampsell teaches readers how to play my new favorite game: WOMB ESCAPE.

—ASH YANG-THOMPSON, author of *Still Worm*

What a strange and wondrous document this book is. Kevin Sampsell's voice is wholly his own—an embodiment of the early 21st century, with its homeless population, its struggles with drugs, its social fabric that somehow still has the innocence of a small village. Within these pages you encounter people beset by the daily sufferings of late-stage, metastatic capitalism. And through it all wanders an impossible baby—a kid who both is and isn't a kid—who is a version of all of us, walking in the moonlit dark. If you like Denis Johnson and Hubert Selby Jr. and the boxes of Joseph Cornell, you will love *Baby in the Night*, Kevin Sampsell's magic, miniature marvel.

—PAULS TOUTONGHI, author of *The Refugee Ocean*

BABY

IN THE

NIGHT

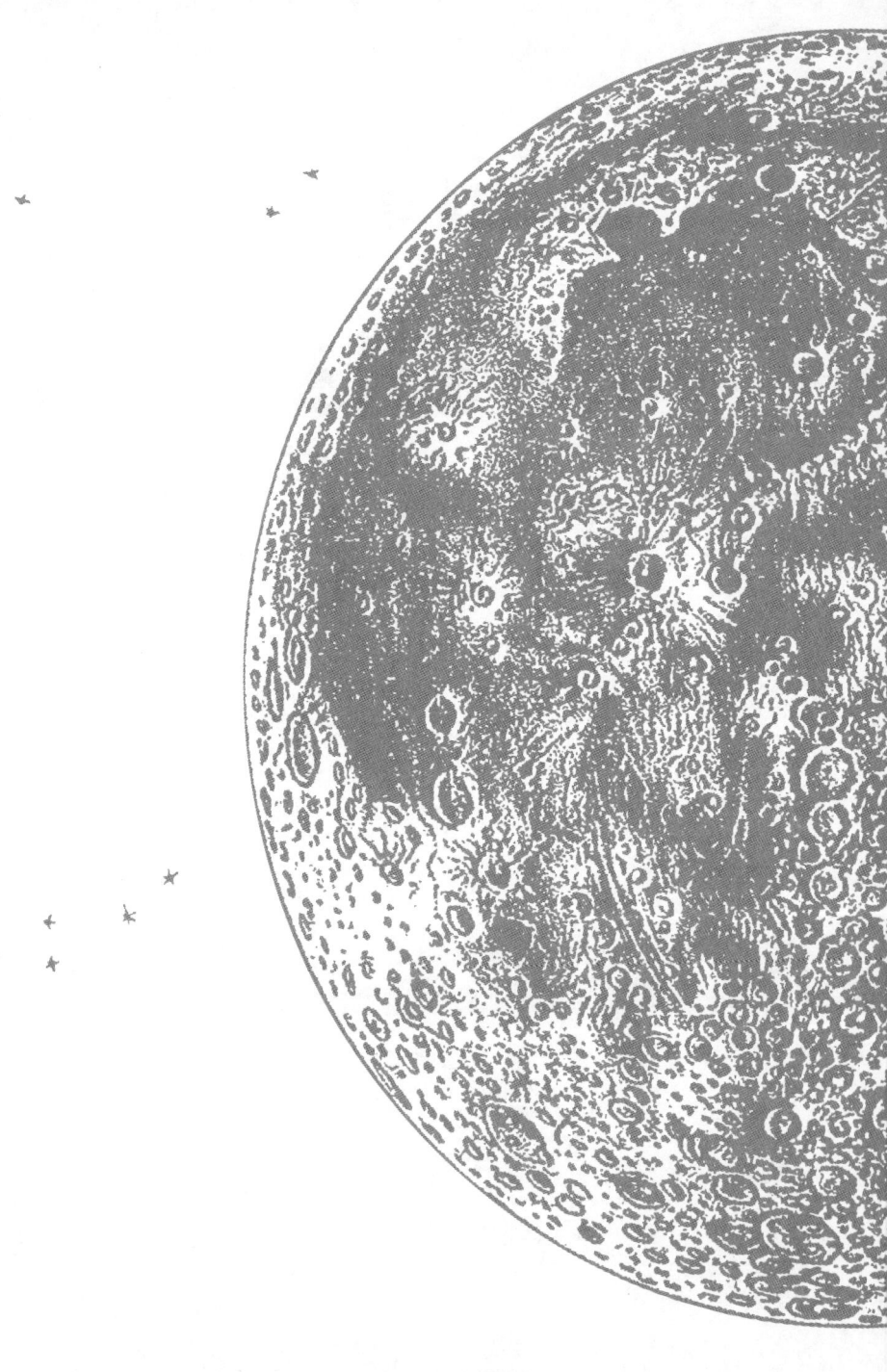

BABY IN THE NIGHT

a novel

KEVIN SAMPSELL

IMPELLER PRESS

PORTLAND, OREGON

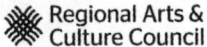
**Regional Arts &
Culture Council**

The author would like to thank the Regional Arts and Culture Council for their generous support in helping this book be completed.

Baby in the Night
Copyright ©2026 Kevin Sampsell
All rights reserved

Cover art, frontispiece, and stars adapted from a woodcut illustration in Agnes Giberne's book *The Story of the Sun, Moon, and Stars* (Cincinnati: National Book Company, 1898). publicdomainreview.org /collection/story-of-sun-moon-stars/

ISBN 978-1-967136-00-1

Impeller Press books are published in Portland, Oregon. We give back 5% of our annual sales to Indigenous communities and individuals to support Indigenous health, creativity, community, and the Landback movement. Please visit landback.org for more information on the Landback movement.

Cover and text design by Patrick Barber
Set in Adobe Kis and DJR Output Sans

Second printing, April 2026
Printed and bound in the United States by Versa Press
Distributed by Asterism Books

impellerpress.com

This book is dedicated to all of my friends.
To all mothers.
To the moon.

TWELVE YEARS OLD

I KNOW PEOPLE don't usually remember their baby years, but I do.

It makes my mom worry. She doesn't think I should remember all the things I remember. Some of them were things she didn't know about, like the giant dog or the boy in the alley, or the droopy face. Or that woman with all her radios playing at the same time. Mom knew about the moon, though, because she kind of started that.

A doctor I go to says I have trauma, which is when bad things happen and you keep thinking about them or when you suddenly remember disturbing things. It wasn't always bad, though. My mom took care of me and didn't want anything to hurt me. She doesn't know where I went on those nights. Or what I saw. Sometimes I remember things from my past and it's really clear, like it'd just happened. And other times it's like a blurry picture.

Sometimes I do feel sad but I know I'm lucky, so I don't think *trauma* is the right word. I don't know if there's a right word for it. Is there a word for believing in magic that no one else can see?

TWO YEARS OLD

1

I WASN'T AFRAID of the dark. Mom always took me out at night, so it seemed normal to me. There were many things different about daytime and nighttime, but I liked them both. They were like two different worlds.

In the daytime world, there were other babies and more colors and people saying nice words and the hot sun that I wasn't supposed to look at.

The nighttime world was dark and endless and there were no other babies and the words people said were loud and strange and I was not allowed to get out of the stroller.

"The darkness is a well that you might fall into," Mom told me once. But I didn't know what a well was.

I liked the nighttime world best, when I thought the moon was just the sun turned into a ball of ice. I could stare at it all I wanted and it didn't hurt my eyes like the sun did.

That was my daddy up there as the moon, shining his moonlight. Sometimes he was huge and grinning, and sometimes smaller and looking away so I couldn't see his face. Some nights he tried to hide, but I could still see a sliver of him.

"Is Daddy like God?" I wanted to ask Mom, but I couldn't say many words yet. Words and sentences and questions were easy in my head, but I didn't know how to use my baby mouth to make all the words come out right. I'd shake my apple bell and

throw my binky instead. I could say a few words: Mom, Daddy, pie, bell, store, park, mine, and no. Sometimes when I said "bell," people thought I was saying "bagel." I was close to mastering "apple," but it sounded too much like "elbow." Maybe I should have gone ahead and said "elbow" to see if it impressed anyone.

Mom kept a notebook with all the words I could say in it. It had a photo of me on the cover and "Tony" in the upper corner. For a long time I didn't know what it said, all those lines and circles. But then I figured out it was my name.

When I couldn't fall asleep at night, Mom pushed me around in my stroller. We lived in a city that was always in the top five for worst crime. I heard someone say this to Mom once, and I wondered if it meant crimes against babies or crimes against grown-ups. One time I saw an old man going pee on a broken refrigerator in an alleyway and then another man came out of the refrigerator swinging a tennis racquet and he beat up the peeing man until he wasn't moving anymore. Then I noticed that the refrigerator didn't have anything in it except a box of baking soda and some baby food splattered all over. I think that's what they meant by "crime."

There were a lot of people outside at night. Some of them lived in tents or boxes on the sidewalk, down the street from our apartment building. Instead of beds, some of them slept in cars, and some of the cars looked like broken toys. There were more of them every night we went out. Mom wheeled me past them without any problem, but sometimes we had to go in the street. "Victims of bad luck" is what she called the sidewalk people.

Mom would sing "Danny Boy" as we rolled by them, but she'd change the words and sing "Tony Boy." Sometimes it was some other lullaby. Maybe something about my daddy, the icy face in the sky. Her songs never put me to sleep, but I did become quiet and calm. I'd stare at all the confused people on the street and smile at them and hiccup and shake the apple bell and say, "Elbow elbow elbow." They acted like they'd never seen a baby at night before, like I was a dream or a ghost or one of those fake babies people use to practice diaper-changing on.

One night I was fussing and crying, and I spooked a skinny old guy with a beard. He tried to spit on me and then fell into a newspaper box. He looked up at my daddy and said, "Fuck you, moon!" I knew that one of those words was a bad word.

Mom laughed at first but grew angry as she pushed me back home. She said she wouldn't take me through that part of the neighborhood at night anymore. Mom could be tough but she cried a lot too. Maybe more than I did. She had long dark hair and skinny arms and a nose so long and awesome that I could never stop looking at it. When she held me in her arms and I fed on her boob milk, I stared right into that nose. It was like looking into a volcano with two holes. I once dreamt I was an explorer walking around the double holes of this volcano and then I fell into the hot lava. I swam in the lava for a long time, and when I climbed out, I had a special super-power: I could turn myself gold.

Mom told me about volcanoes once because that's my middle name: Volcano. For a while I wasn't sure what my mom's name was. It could have been Jennie or Baby or Mom. Not all of them at once, though. People just picked one and said it. I was always confused when people called my mom "Baby." I was the baby, not her. She was too big to be a baby. I said the word *baby*, and she added it to my list of words. B-A-B-Y.

Mom started taking me to a different neighborhood at night. I guess it was all right, but I missed the sounds and smells of the one we used to go to—all the voices and music and the way the air smelled like smoke. This place smelled like trees and baby powder. It was as quiet as trees and baby powder too. Sometimes the air blew by and it sounded like a softly strummed guitar.

To tell you the truth, I was bored with this other neighborhood. I made a fuss and threw my binky and my apple bell. She pushed me faster as if that would calm me down. I heard her heavy breathing and I knew she was mad by the way she was gripping the handle of my stroller so hard. I felt the tension flowing through her. I imagined that she could crush the handle in her hands. It would crumble like a pretzel between her tight fingers. I wanted a pretzel that night. I wished I could say the word *pretzel*.

"Presso," I said. "Presso!" I screamed as loud as I could, which was pretty loud. I saw some lights turning on around us. People were waking up.

"It's two o'clock in the morning!" someone shouted from a window. "Shut up your baby!"

The next day I had a playdate at Tater's house. He was three—a little bit older than me. He knew how to say "pretzel" and "milkshake" and a lot more words than I could. His mom used to make him milkshakes from her boob milk. I once had a taste of one, and it was pretty good. I liked Tater's mom. She had a big nose too.

I wanted to tell Tater about my nighttime strolls. I wanted to know if he went outside at night with his mom too. We were playing on his floor with wood blocks and toy cars and fake babies and pretend food. Tater took a plastic banana and a fake hammer and one of the fake babies and told me to watch. He dragged his big dollhouse over to show me what they did in their house at night. I could tell he thought it was really great, but I lost interest pretty fast. I looked around Tater's room for any new toys or something to put in my mouth.

"Hey!" Tater said. "Hey! Hey! Look at how they sleep."

I looked in the dollhouse and saw the banana, hammer, and baby side by side on a tiny bed.

"My mommy sleeps like this," he said, and then he turned the banana over and over. The hammer got knocked off the bed. The baby tumbled off the bed. Then the banana snored.

"Be *your* mom," Tater said.

He held out the plastic banana, but I looked at it and shook my head. It didn't look like my mom. I grabbed it anyway and made the banana walk around the outside of the house.

Tater got impatient and said, "Make your mom sleep." But I didn't really know how Mom slept, if she even slept much at all. Some nights, I saw her open the curtains and stare out at my daddy in the sky for a long time. She'd tell me stories about him at bedtime.

"Daddy," I said to Tater, holding the fake banana. If it were real, I would've peeled it. I would have taken a handful and squished it into the shape of the moon. I would've held it up above the dollhouse so it would be my pretend daddy. I would've eaten the rest of the banana and laid the empty peel on the toy bed.

That night, Mom went somewhere and left me with a babysitter. The babysitter was a girl named Brandy, and all she did was eat ice cream and text with her boyfriend. The TV was on even though it wasn't supposed to be, and there were policemen on the screen driving around at night in a neighborhood that looked like mine. I pretended to be playing with Lego pieces on the floor but kept getting distracted by the TV. There was a woman with bright red lipstick who looked like a woman with bright lipstick I'd seen before. There was a man wearing a dirty baseball cap holding a cardboard sign who looked familiar. There was an alleyway with rats around the garbage cans that seemed like an alley we lived by. There was a tipped-over refrigerator, and there was a man with a gun and an angry look on his face. He was hiding from the police. The TV showed the police driving slowly, looking for him. They showed the man again. Then the police again. I wondered why *I* could see the man but the police couldn't. I felt anxious.

There was a close-up of the gun in the man's hand. Then a close-up of the policemen's shoes. A rat ran by and made a noise. Even though most people are scared of rats, I kind of get excited when I see a rat on the street. It's like seeing an imaginary friend. Unless it starts chasing me.

"You shouldn't be watching this," Brandy said. She picked up the remote control and aimed it at the screen. Right before the screen went black, I heard the music on the show getting louder. It turned into a spike whistling through the air, and then they showed my daddy. He was bright white against the dark sky and his face looked warped and hurt.

Brandy picked me up and I started to cry. I wanted to go save Daddy. Brandy carried me to my room and tucked me in as I squirmed. I pointed at the window and said, "Daddy Daddy Daddy." She opened the curtain a little, but I couldn't see Daddy.

"It's time for bed now. Time to go to sleep," Brandy said. I sat in the dark by myself and tried to stop crying. I heard the TV come back on with the volume turned lower. I wished Daddy could talk, but I didn't know what he sounded like. I listened for a long time, and then someone was telling jokes and laughter was coming out of the TV, but it didn't make me feel better.

Eventually, I crawled over the wood rail that was meant to keep me from falling out of bed. This was the big-boy bed

Mom gave me after my crib. It was new and looked like a red wagon. I walked out to the front room. Brandy was still there but had fallen asleep. I looked at the clock and it said 1, 2, 3, 4, 5, 6, and some other numbers. I wasn't sure what clocks meant yet or why people kept looking at them.

I was wet. I went into the bathroom and took my diaper off. It felt good to be naked. Sometimes I wished we could all live naked—me, Mom, Tater, Tater's mom, the policemen on TV. I walked out of the bathroom naked and stood in front of Brandy. I watched her breathing and turning over, this way and that, like the banana. I went to the door and turned the knob. The door opened and I looked down the long hallway of our apartment building. I saw the door at the end. I saw the nighttime.

Before I could make my move, I had to put on some clothes. First, I looked for a new diaper, but I couldn't figure out where they were. I'd just started wearing this kind called Pull-Ups, which were big-boy diapers. I couldn't figure out where they were, but I found a plastic bag full of smaller diapers and I carefully put one on. I wished I didn't have to wear one, but I was potty training and hadn't figured out how to pee straight or why it was even important to do that. For a long time I thought all people wore Pull-Ups and toilets were like garbage cans but with water inside. I thought bathrooms were places where grown-ups went to sit and read when they were angry.

I put on my new Thomas the Tank Engine T-shirt and Velcro-strap shoes. I especially liked this shirt because Daddy was on it too. Thomas was smiling and going down a train track, and my dad was right over him, shaped like a sliver and surrounded by stars. I grabbed a paper bag and put some food in it and some markers, my apple bell, and a toy cell phone in case I needed it. I used to have a gun, but I think Mom took it away. She said guns are for bullies.

Once I entered the outside, I realized it was a lot different when you're by yourself and not protected by a stroller. A desperate-looking man with red hair and pimples all over his face and arms asked me if I had any spare change, and then he blinked at me a bunch of times until his expression totally changed.

"What's wrong with you?" he said. "You used to be cool but now you look like some kind of alien."

I didn't know what he was talking about, so I pointed to my shirt. "Daddy," I said, poking myself in the chest.

"Whatever," he said, and grabbed my bag from me. He pulled out a plastic cup of pudding and ripped the foil off the top and smelled it. I said, "Mine!" but could only watch as he shook a big glob of it into his mouth. I worried about my food. What if I ran out? What if I starved?

"These are my favorite cookies," the man said, finding and eating my Oreos. It made me so angry that I wanted to fight him.

"Ookies! Mine!" I screamed up at him, and though I couldn't reach his throat, I flailed my arms as hard as I could all over his diaper area and made him spit black-and-white slobbery crumbs on the sidewalk.

"You freaky-ass bastard!" he yelled as I picked up my bag and ran away. A couple of people stared at me and pointed as I scampered to the next block. I searched for the policemen I saw on TV but couldn't find them. I looked in the sky and didn't see my daddy either. I spun in a circle, looking up. I walked over to an old parking lot on the corner where the sky wasn't blocked as much. There were a couple of cars parked there that looked like they'd been there for a long time. They had flat tires and broken windows. I searched the sky again, trying to find the moon.

In one of the stories Mom used to tell me, she explained why Daddy went on vacation sometimes. She said he had to go to the other side of the world and shine on other children who needed love too. "Daddy has a lot of love to give" is what she said. She always said it with a sad smile though.

I heard other babies had dads who were real grown-ups, but I didn't believe it at first. Sometimes I saw guys at the park who could have been daddies. I tugged on Mom 's dress and pointed at one man and said "Daddy?" And she said, "Yes, that's Maggie's daddy. He is a bus driver." And then I pointed at another one and asked again, "Daddy?" And she said, "That's Roger. He's Rafael's daddy. He works at the hospital." I kept an eye on those daddies. I saw them chasing their kids through the play structure, pushing them on the swings, cutting crusts off sandwiches. I sometimes wondered if those daddies could be my daddy. What was my dad doing up there, anyway? Sometimes I wished he were a bus driver or a hospital worker instead of a moon.

I was walking through the dark parking lot when I saw a shadow walking toward me. It was a woman with a lot of skin showing, and the clothes she had on looked like underwear. She looked like a woman I saw in one of my mom's magazines once, with so much big hair like a beautiful lion. She had pretty skin and her shoes were very tall. I noticed that she had a limp and a Band-Aid on her arm.

"Hey, baby," she said, looking at me strangely. "What are you doing with that thing?" She reached down and grabbed my diaper and ripped it off me. Part of me felt scared, but part of me felt happy to be half naked.

A man wearing shiny clothes came over and said, "What are you doing, Nikki? Is this your baby?"

"No," the woman said, lighting a cigarette, "but he had a maxi pad stuck to him. You gonna call the cops?"

The man shot her a look like she was crazy and then stopped another woman walking by. "Hey, grandma. Call the cops on this baby here or go buy it a diaper, or take it to the pound or something."

"Fuck you," the woman said. "I'm only thirty-eight, and I'm working."

As they argued, I walked away quickly and kept my eyes on the sky. I heard one of them shout, "That baby's getting away!"

They couldn't catch me, though, because I was too fast. I was probably the fastest baby in town. Mom used to be a track star, and she said I could even beat *her* in a race.

I found the alleyway I saw on TV earlier and hid in the shadows until I thought it was safe to come out. I crept out from behind a dumpster and almost tripped over a guy slouching against the wall with some kind of big rubber band wrapped around his arm. He looked like a teenager and his hair was green, standing out like neon in the darkness.

"Holy shit," he said. "Are you real?"

For some reason, I liked him right away, so I stood there, half naked, and tried to use new words.

"I'm Tony," I said. Then I said my full name: "Tony Volcano Ventura." I emptied the plastic bag I had with me and gave him my apple bell. "Apple bell," I said.

"Apple bell," he said back.

"Shake it," I said. He did, and we laughed. He looked at the apple bell like he was trying to figure out where the sound was coming from. There was a painted face on it—big eyes and a smiley mouth with a little tongue sticking out. The young man was looking at the mouth like he might see inside it.

"You're not a fake baby, are you? Like a cop?" he asked. He shifted a little and I saw something attached to his arm, like he was giving himself a shot. I wondered if he worked at a hospital.

"I'm looking for a man with a gun," I said. "And I'm looking for Daddy too."

The young man was confused, and I was too. How did I

know how to say words like an adult? His eyes were closing.

"This has been really fun," he said, handing the apple bell back to me. "Good night."

"But wait," I said. "This is what my dad looks like." I pointed to my shirt.

"Your dad looks like Thomas the Tank Engine?"

"No, right here." I poked myself in the chest.

"The moon!" he said, and he looked around the best he could, craning his neck this way and that way. "He was here last night," he said. Then he wagged his finger at me like he was teaching me something and said, "He's not out every night. Sometimes he's on vacation."

Suddenly I saw a swirl of lights coming from a car turning into the alley. I tried to escape, but before I got out of the alley, I stumbled over a pair of pants someone had left on the ground. A police car rolled up to me and made a *whoop-whoop* sound. It was the policemen from the TV. They looked at me and smiled and the driver said, "You must be the runaway baby."

There was no baby seat in the car, so the policeman who wasn't driving had to hold me in his lap in the backseat. They were asking me questions, but I didn't have all the right words to answer them. I was back to "mom," "mine," and "elbow."

We pulled up to the apartment and Mom was waiting outside, upset and crying. I saw a small bright orb in the sky. It looked farther away than usual and there was a thin cloud slowly drifting in front of it, changing its color from white to silver. The soft glow made me feel safe. It winked at me.

2

I HEARD MOM tell someone she had to fire Brandy. I was scared when I heard that because I thought it had something to do with real fire, and I know that fire can burn people. But fire can also mean not having to see someone anymore. I felt a little bad about it, but it wasn't my fault that she fell asleep when she was supposed to be babysitting.

I got the feeling that Mom didn't trust me after that night, like I'd fooled her pretty bad, like I'd had the whole thing planned. I was just worried about Daddy and wanted to make sure he was okay. I saw the gun on TV and I got worried. I knew he was far away in the sky, but I thought maybe a gun shooting bullets could still reach him. If someone with a gun flew an airplane up there, they might be able to shoot him. I hadn't been on an airplane yet, but I once dreamed about being on one. I wanted to go up really high and get close enough to wave at Daddy and maybe touch his face.

Mom was feeding me as I thought about guns and airplanes and Daddy. She was sweating a little bit and I could taste salt in her boob milk. It tasted different but it was still good. Maybe something was changing in my mouth. I had some teeth but I wasn't sure what they did yet, besides hurting really bad sometimes. I hated falling asleep while Mom fed me because it was one of my favorite times of the day. I tried to stay awake, so I'd make up stories in my head about her tattoos.

There was one of a giraffe that went up her arm so that its neck bent when Mom moved her arm. Above the giraffe's head was a rocket ship that was pointing up. Both of these tattoos wrapped around her arm so you couldn't really see the whole thing at once. I wondered who was in the rocket ship and if the giraffe had ever ridden in it.

Mom had five other tattoos: her momma's name in a heart on her shoulder, a scary-looking bug called a scorpion on her wrist, a fat baby named Buddha on her leg, a sunrise on her back, and on her chest some words from a sad song we listened to sometimes in the car when Mom wanted to go fast on the highway and cry.

Later, we were at Crown Thrift, which was the store Mom worked at. She was like a boss because she had her own office and had to do a lot of writing and math. She took me to work with her on Wednesdays and Fridays, and I always had new toys to play with because they sold toys and Mom said I could test them. They also sold shirts, pants, books, TVs, dishes, shoes, and things I didn't know the names of. A lot of people came into the store every day, and sometimes they bought things and sometimes they'd ask for the bathroom and sometimes they'd test the couches by taking a nap on them. One time a man came in with a live monkey and tried to sell it to the store. Mom didn't know what to say to the guy, and then he yelled at her about his rights. The police had to come and get him. I still wonder if the monkey went to jail with that man.

"I have to do some work, my little volcano," Mom said. She put me down on a blanket on her office floor and told me I could go to dreamland if I was sleepy. My stomach felt like it was blowing bubbles from my breakfast oatmeal, and it made me burp. I wiped my mouth off, and Mom smiled down at me because I was getting to be a big boy and she didn't have to wipe my face as much as she used to. I laughed and burped more until my tummy felt good enough to take a nap.

I was having a dream about sheep turning into rainclouds when I was woken up by the sound of Mom crying. Someone kept calling her "baby," and she was trying to cover his mouth with her hand. It was Ben, a man Mom worked with and called her "special friend." Even though he was special and hung out with us at home too, he wasn't my dad. I heard her say his name and kept my eyes closed.

"Oh, Ben," she said, and it sounded different from any other names I'd heard her say. It reminded me of the sound of the apple bell. The clang of it, the excitement. One time I saw a man at a carnival swing a hammer down on a big button and a red ball shot straight up and smacked a shiny bell on top. I thought about that sound all the time. It wasn't super loud but it was firm and certain, like a fact. Mom said Ben's name like that—a red ball striking a giant bell.

I'm not sure why Mom spent time with Ben and would sometimes let him kiss her. I wondered if Daddy knew, if he could see. Ben tried to act nice to me, but I didn't trust him. Once when we were all eating dinner, he took a fish stick off my plate and ate it when Mom wasn't looking.

I pretended I was still asleep, but opened my eyes to see why Mom was crying. She looked over at me and I closed my eyes quickly, but I could tell she was still looking at me because she made a *shhh* sound and it got quiet.

"I think he's waking up," she said.

I heard Ben shift around and knock something over. I could tell he was tiptoeing closer to me, crouching down.

"He's fine," he whispered. "Give me his pacifier."

I opened one eye partway and saw Mom clean my binky off with her spit and give it to Ben. He awkwardly inserted it between my lips. I gave it a couple of convincing sucks and waited for them to keep talking.

The sounds I heard were vaguely familiar, like good-night kisses but slower. I heard Mom say, "Touch me, baby," and it startled me so much that my eyes popped open to see if there was another baby somewhere. At first, I was excited, thinking I might have a playdate, but I didn't see anyone except Mom and Ben pushing a filing cabinet against the wall. They were breathing hard, like the filing cabinet was really heavy.

"I love it when you call me baby," Ben said.

I spat out my binky and cried as loud as I could.

3

I FELT HELPLESS and confused for the next several days. I wondered if there was another baby. But I figured out it was just a word people said sometimes, especially on the radio. There were a lot of songs about babies.

Mom didn't take me out at night as much as she had before, but I could still see Daddy through my window sometimes. I wanted to get out there again so he could see me too.

At Tater's house one day, we were playing with his big cardboard blocks. They looked like bricks, and we were making walls. Tater was better at stacking them up than I was. He probably could have been a professional wall builder. I could only balance the stack as tall as my head and then they'd fall over. I couldn't figure out what I was doing wrong. But Tater stacked them higher than his head, and then he stood on his stool and made it even higher. Then he got down and said, "Watch me."

I watched him as he backed up a few steps, staring at the blocks as if they were a bad guy in a movie. Then he made a monster sound, like a roar and a growl, and he ran and crashed, shoulder first, into the wall of blocks. He flailed his arms up as he made contact and the fake bricks flew up like they were exploding all over the place. It was one of the coolest things I'd ever seen.

Tater had a look on his face like he'd hurt himself, but he was also laughing. For about two seconds I peed myself with excitement and shouted a new word: "Boom!" Tater laughed more, and I said, "Mine! Boom!" because I wanted to run and crash too.

"Okay," said Tater. "But I have to make it."

He quickly built another wall and said, "Don't get hurt." I got nervous when he said that, and it was like he could tell, so he said, "I'll show you." He stepped back and then acted like he was running in slow motion at the blocks. "You have to go fast to break the wall," he said, "and then you boom!"

I must have still looked worried because Tater grabbed my hand and said, "Let's do it together. To make us stronger."

I nodded at him to show that I was ready. It was a nod I copied from Mom when she'd tell me about a rule I had to follow. She'd look me straight in the eyes and give me that nod and say, "You with me?" And I'd do the same nod back.

Sometimes I noticed when she talked to other people, she would do a nod with them too, but it was different. It wasn't as soft. It wasn't like warm eyes locking in with their eyes. And not like superglue that they knew would never let go. Her nod to other people wasn't life and death and all the minutes and days and years that she looked forward to with them. It wasn't like they were on a special team with her. That nod was just a regular nod.

But when Mom nodded at me, it was our special nod, and I would smile and say, "Mom," and nod back, like a little mirror.

Tater held my hand and said, "Okay. Go when I say three. Ready?"

I thought about it for a second and got prepared. I knew how to count to three, so I was ready.

"One, two, three!" he said quickly, and we ran and jumped into the blocks. It reminded me of the one time I was in a bouncy castle at the Choo-Choo Cheese Pizza Place. I was a flying superhero, in charge of the world around me and protected from all things bad. The world should have more bouncy castles.

Tater let go of my hand when we hit the ground and the blocks scattered all around us. One block bounced off something and hit me in the face, but I was tough and pretended it was no big deal.

"Are you okay?" Tater asked.

I managed to say, "Uh-huh."

"That was just like jail," he said. "We broke out of the jail."

It made me think maybe we *could* be a breaking-out team. Maybe I could learn more words, and we could make a plan and break out at night and see my dad together. We had done sleepovers before. And Tater was older than me and bigger. Maybe people would think we were brothers and then the police wouldn't pick us up.

I felt a sharp pain in my right arm when I tried to get up. My arm felt like a twisty straw. I moaned really loud and heard Tater's mom run up the stairs to see what was wrong. She opened the door and I saw her face turn white.

"Tater, what happened?" she asked with a shaky voice.

Tater started crying, so I sucked in my breath and answered her question.

"Jail," I said.

4

MOM WAS CRYING when she got to the hospital, and then she looked mad for a while, and then she and the doctor were talking and she was laughing at all his dumb jokes. I don't think I had ever seen her moods change so much. I was more worried about her than anyone seemed about me. They said I had a fracture in my right wrist. It hurt a lot when they touched it, but getting so much attention at the hospital was pretty cool. I tried to say the word *fracture* when the doctor showed it to us on the X-ray, but it sounded like I was saying "fact shoe."

The doctor put a red dot on my wrist where it was broken and told me it would be healed in a few weeks. I had a hard time imagining the little black line on the X-ray was on a tiny bone under my skin and that it made me feel so bad. Two nurses put a cast on my arm, covering up the red mark the doctor had made. They smelled like Lucky Charms and kept saying that I was a brave boy. They wore shirts with cartoon characters I didn't recognize on them. They must have been from cable channels.

I chose pink wrap to go around the cast because I thought it might be the easiest color for my dad to see from up in the sky. Mom wanted me to pick blue, but I didn't think Daddy would see that color in the dark. I pouted when they showed me the other colors, so Mom let me get pink.

When they were done, I got to sit in a little wheelchair as the nurses drew pictures on my cast. Mom and Tater's mom were talking to each other in the waiting room, and I worried that I wouldn't get to play with Tater for a long time. Tater's dad came to pick him up at the hospital, and I felt embarrassed and dumb when I saw him. He asked Tater if he was okay, and then he leaned down and told me I'd have to do high fives with my left hand now.

Before we left the hospital, Tater's mom kissed me on the cheek and said she was sorry for some reason. But it wasn't anyone's fault. She wasn't in jail with me and Tater.

Mom was talking to the doctor before they wheeled me out. I noticed her acting all serious. She was leaning in toward him like she was going to fall over, or maybe she was going to pretend to fall. I wondered if she would make a fracture in her wrist so she could get a cast from him too.

Sometimes I got jealous that Tater had a dad. He had a job doing something in the forest and brought home cool rocks and flowers and pieces of wood all the time. He still lived with them and was even there at night, sleeping in his bed. All Tater had to do was walk down the hall and open his mom and dad's bedroom door and he could see them both—even climb into bed with them if he wanted to.

I could tell that Tater's dad is his dad because they looked alike. They had the same eyes and even the same messy hair. Sometimes I looked up at Daddy and I couldn't tell if we looked alike at all. I tried to shape my mouth like his. I touched my face and wondered what his skin felt like, if it was smooth or bumpy. I wanted to know if he'd ever cracked a bone.

5

I DIDN'T KNOW how hard it would be to eat with just one hand. I couldn't hold anything very well using my cast hand. It started to tingle if I did, and not in a fun way. I was eating a muffin with one hand, and it broke apart all over my face. I usually held it with both hands and it would stay together better, but the way I had to do it with a cast was really complicated and messy. It was hard to aim for my mouth with only one hand. Mom had to cut the muffin into pieces for me. Grapes were cut in half like I was a one-year-old, cheese sandwiches were cut into tiny squares, and even my cookies were broken up, which was really upsetting for me. I was eating and crying a little at the same time. Mom tried to help by feeding me, making train sounds with a spoon as she fit my lunch perfectly into my mouth, just like old times.

I hoped she would give me her nipple too. I wanted to save room for milk. But she hadn't given me any for a few days. She said something about how I was getting too old to feed from her. She said she had to wing me. I wasn't sure what that meant. Was I going to grow wings like those babies on the calendar at Mom's work? I thought that would be cool. Maybe having wings would make up for my big clunky cast arm. I didn't think Tater had been winged yet. I'd seen him getting milk from his mom before. He always kept one eye open and one closed, like he wanted to make sure his mom didn't switch her nipple with a bottle or binky, which is a trick that moms do sometimes. Sometimes he looked around at other stuff or watched TV with his open eye while she fed him.

I know now that she was saying *wean* and it didn't have anything to do with wings. It means your mom is going to run out of milk for you. Then you have to get it from cows, which costs money and doesn't taste as good.

"Come over here, poor guy," Mom said. She lifted me up and unsnapped part of her shirt. She positioned me carefully so my cast didn't get in the way. I think she felt sorry for me because her voice sounded especially cartoonish, the way it got when she saw other people's babies. Tater called it "baby talk," but for some reason it reminded me of balloons bouncing around and being happy. I wanted to call it "balloon talk."

"You and Tater, always finding trouble," she said. She leaned over and kissed my cast. Maybe if she would have done that before we went to the hospital it would have made it better and I wouldn't have needed a cast. But maybe that didn't work for serious injuries like fractures. It worked on other things, though, like when I got poked by a thorn and blood came out of my finger. She kissed it and made it feel better, but it kept bleeding, so she put a Band-Aid on it and kissed it a thousand more times for two days, and then she took the Band-Aid off and it was like the thorn had never touched me. My finger was like new. Magic does work sometimes.

"I better keep an eye on you boys," Mom said as she fed me. "Before I know it, you two will be smoking cigarettes, robbing ice cream trucks, and making girls cry."

This made me feel sad for many reasons, and I stopped sucking for a moment because I was confused. For one thing, smoking involved fire, and I was pretty scared of fire. And I didn't know why I would make girls cry. It's not nice to make anyone cry. Unless she took my Hot Wheels and threw them in the stickery bushes or something. I might make a girl cry if she did that.

The ice cream truck idea sounded fun. So really the only part that seemed weird is the smoking cigarettes thing.

"You all done, champ?" Mom asked. She set me down in my stroller and I stretched out, feeling the good kind of tingle go from my head to my toes. It was the feeling I got before I fell asleep for a nap.

"Wanna go for a stroll?" Mom asked. I blinked a yes at her nice and slow.

I loved having a stroll during naptime. It was so peaceful, like I was an astronaut floating down the street in a rocket made of blankets. But people kept stopping us this time.

"What happened?" they asked.

I kept saying, "Jail," but Mom got all technical and said some doctor words, and then the people wanted to sign my cast or draw a picture on it. "I'm not a coloring book!" I wanted to yell. But after a couple of people drew some fun stuff like cats and stars and hearts, I kind of liked how it looked.

"Cool," I said.

"Did you say 'cool'?" Mom asked.

"Cool," I said louder.

She laughed and took out her notebook and wrote the word in there. Then she wrote COOL on my cast.

As we strolled around the neighborhood, I looked for signs of the night. I saw people sleeping on the sidewalk and in the park and in their cars, and I wondered if any of them had stuffies to cuddle with. I had four main stuffies: a striped tiger, a brown bear, a raccoon, and a turtle that I used as a pillow sometimes. I used to have five stuffies, but I threw up on one of them and then made it fly through the car window. I still miss it, even though I don't know what it was. Mom called him Squid.

The sun was hotter than usual on this day. I hoped it wasn't too hot for the people who were always outside. I thought about the boy with the green hair as Mom pushed me past the alleyway. I decided to throw my apple bell out of the stroller so she would have to stop. It rolled between a couple of garbage cans. I leaned forward in my stroller and shouted, "Alpo alpo alpo!" My mouth was so close to saying *apple* the right way. I heard a sound come from the alleyway, but it wasn't my friend with the green hair. It was a man with a big belly and a shopping cart full of cans and bottles and a radio with a bunch of wires coming out. He limped by us and pushed his cart across the street, making a car honk its horn at him.

"Oh, you silly goose," Mom said as she retrieved the apple bell. She picked it up and wiped it off with her shirt and held it in front of my face. "Do you want to throw this away? Is that what you want?" She looked serious when she said it, and I started to worry.

"No," I said.

She pointed at the garbage cans with the apple bell and I heard it clang like it knew what was happening too. It didn't want to be thrown away to die in a garbage can. My panic matched its clanging sound, and Mom said, "This is only made of plastic, and it will break if you throw it on the sidewalk."

I saw a bad scratch on the face on the apple, right between the eyes, and I reached out to grab it with my one good hand.

"You don't get to play with your toys if you're going to break them, okay?" she said. "This toy would make another little boy very happy." She placed it in the stroller, underneath my seat, where she kept our bag of snacks.

I heard the sound of its bell rolling around inside of it as we continued down the sidewalk and I hoped I hadn't hurt it too badly. I put a Band-Aid on the scratch when we got home.

6

I REMEMBER WHEN I first learned to walk. Mom called my aunt Maria and said, "Better come over quick because this cowboy is determined to start walking today."

Maria made it over quick, and she and Mom watched me like a kid watches a wind-up toy, waiting for it to move. They sat on our living room carpet, which felt like fur and was the same color as the almond milk Mom put in her coffee every day. Maria and Mom sat a little bit apart, facing each other and keeping their arms out as I wobbled on my legs between them.

I made my brain tell one leg to move forward. Then I told it to move the other leg. And then maybe my brain forgot about the first leg, because I tipped over and fell on my butt. I was trying to walk for the first time, but I was just falling down for the first time. I guess that's always the order of it.

Each time I plopped, Mom picked me right back up and I'd try again. They clapped and chanted my name: "TO-NY! TO-NY! TO-NY!" It was actually making me more nervous, but at the same time it was really exciting. My baby muscles were happy, like the times I got to go in the swimming pool with Mom. And yeah, I know a lot of babies don't have muscles, but I did. Mom said so.

After falling on my butt a hundred times that day, I was getting tired, but I was also starting to figure out how to balance better. If I put my right arm straight in front of me and bent my left arm up like I was pointing to the sky, I stood pretty solid. If I stopped thinking about my legs so much and pretended like I was crawling, but on my feet instead of my knees, I would move forward a little. I walked two steps, and they went crazy cheering and laughing. I'd never seen Mom look so proud.

Somebody knocked on our apartment door and asked if everything was okay. It was the old guy next door. He had white crazy hair and a wooden cane that looked like an umbrella with the top part cut off. Mom told him I was learning how to walk, and I felt a little angry for a second. What did she mean, *learning*? I had walked two steps at least three times now. I was walking—for real!

She invited him in, and now there were three of them— Mom, Maria, and whatever this neighbor guy's name was— and they were all clapping and chanting, and I was trying to be cool in front of this neighbor, like "No big deal," and I walked five steps! I was actually impressed with myself. The neighbor guy was even crying, and I thought he'd hurt himself somehow, but maybe he was sad because he had to walk with a cane and now I was better at walking than him. I kind of wished I had a cool cane like his, though.

I was getting pretty tired and grabbed at Mom's shirt so I could relax and be fed without all the noise and attention. The neighbor said sorry for interrupting my big moment but thanks for letting him stay and watch, and then he wrote down his phone number for Mom in case she ever needed anything. His hand was shaking so much that the number he wrote down looked like a game of tic-tac-toe.

After he left I heard Maria ask Mom something about Daddy. They were kind of whispering, like secret talk, so I closed my eyes and pretended to be asleep. I heard Mom say,

"I wish things were different. But I guess everyone says that."

"A father should see his son's first steps," Maria said.

"I know," said Mom. "But there are plenty of other steps to come."

It's funny to think back on those days when I began walking. I thought I was pretty fancy but I actually wasn't. I heard my doctor tell Mom that I was a little late to the walking thing and that most toddlers are walking or trying to walk around the age of one. Sixteen months was unusual but not really a bad thing, she said.

It didn't seem long before I could run and walk backwards and jump. It's weird in a way because in my head I'd always been able to do those things even when my body wasn't ready. I'd just crawl everywhere. Crawling was fun, like I was a turtle or a dog. I kind of miss crawling.

The baby doctor I saw sometimes was Dr. Duck-Duck. I'm not sure if that was her real name, though. Mom always tried to sound excited when she said we were going to see Dr. Duck-Duck.

Sometimes good things happened, and other times bad things happened when I saw Dr. Duck-Duck. One time I had to get shots poked in me—one for something called polio and another for hippopotamus disease and then some other things with numbers and letters I can't remember. The one that hurt the most was for chicken pox, but I thought they said "chicken boxes." I spent the rest of that day scared of becoming a chicken in a box.

The good times at Dr. Duck-Duck's were really fun, though. The nurses wore funny hats and always gave me a toy before we left. They said I was a special boy and that I should always be myself and be proud of who I am.

One time Dr. Duck-Duck tapped my knees with a little

hammer, and it surprised me and somehow made me kick my leg out. It was like a magic trick. Then she let me do it to her, and she kicked her leg too. It was so funny. She made a sound like *bonk!* And I said it too. "Bonk! Bonk! Bonk!"

My favorite day at Dr. Duck-Duck's was when we played Simon Says and then had a dance contest. She said she wanted to see my moves, so she turned on her phone and a bunch of different kinds of songs filled the room, and I had to dance slow and then fast and then funny and then copycat her.

"Mashed potato!" she said, and I looked around to see if there was a mashed potato somewhere because I love mashed potatoes, but she said it was something you do with your legs and feet, so I did what she did until the song changed to "The Twist" and we did that for a minute. Mom was cracking up and clapping her hands like she does whenever I danced.

I like mashed potatoes with butter and cheese and sour cream, and sometimes I like them with gravy and sometimes with almond butter and applesauce. I wanted Mom and Dr. Duck-Duck to talk more about mashed potatoes.

The main things Mom and Dr. Duck-Duck talked about, though, were the walking and talking. I felt the same way about talking that I did about walking. It was like my brain really wanted to but my mouth didn't know how yet or maybe just didn't try hard enough. Whenever I heard words, I could learn them in my head but not my mouth. Even complicated words like *milkshake* or *hippopotamus* sat in my head for a long time before coming out. I tried to say "milkshake" when we were at Wendy's once. It was right by Crown Thrift and Mom knew I liked the chicken nuggets, so we would go there when I'd been especially good. I was trying to say "milkshake," but it sounded like "mushy." I ran over to the straws and grabbed one and said "mushy" a bunch of times until she figured out what I was saying.

"I'll get a small one that we can share," she said.

After we got our food, we took it to Crown Thrift and I tried to drink the milkshake, but it was too thick and wouldn't even come through the straw. I tried to drink it straight from the cup, but it didn't move, so I got mad and made a lot of angry sounds. Mom said, "You have to use the spoon, little cutie."

She took the red plastic spoon and airplaned some of the milkshake into my mouth. But it wasn't like a real milkshake, and I scrunched up my face because I thought she was playing a trick on me. Grown-ups were always playing food tricks. They eat something like green beans or pineapple and pretend like it was the best thing in the world, and then they give you some and it tastes like a gross crayon.

"You don't like the Frosty?" Mom said.

"What the heck is a Frosty?" I wanted to say, but for some reason I said, "What da Fraa?" It was the first time I said "what." It felt special, like an important word I could say anytime. Mom took out her notebook and wrote it down.

She was laughing about something. "You better watch your little mouth there, guy," she said.

Later that day I found a mirror in Mom's purse and quietly watched my mouth, waiting for it to do something.

7

I HADN'T HAD a babysitter in a long time, and at night I could see Daddy through my window, but he seemed cold and bored, like he didn't know I was watching him. I wanted to talk to him, maybe show him how I could do the Mashed Potato with my legs, and I wanted to show him my new toy that shines in the dark like he did. It was shaped like a scary bat and lit up if you squeezed where its butt was. I thought it would be cool to light up like that at night because there were some streets that were dark and hard to see on.

I decided he was going to be my friend when I broke out that night. I named him Ray.

Mom kept looking in my room to check on me, but I pretended to be asleep. I was pretending so much that I actually did get sleepy. Finally I heard the TV turn off, then water splashing in the bathroom sink, and then her footsteps walking by my room and into her room. I knew they were her footsteps because I'd memorized them. Even before I was born, I knew them like you might know a song. You might think that's weird but it's true.

I looked out my window and watched Daddy's face to see if he might give me some sort of sign. There was a cloud slowly moving in front of him, and I decided that when the cloud was all the way past, I'd make my move. Watching the cloud move was like when I saw Tater's dad sucking on a pipe once. He would open his mouth and circles made of smoke would float out, and he'd close his mouth again and open it real quick, and another circle would shoot out and go through the circle he just made. Then he'd smile and wink at us like this was some kind of secret message and only we knew what it meant.

Daddy's smoke was just a wavy cloud, though, passing over the bottom of his face. For some reason it also made me think of taking a bath and putting my chin and mouth and nose in the water. I had to hold my breath when I did that because all water has a breathing and a not-breathing side. You can't breathe *under* water so that's where the not-breathing side is. Above the water is the breathing side, where you can't drown because there's air.

I watched the cloud finally disappear from Daddy's face and then I got my bag of stuff and headed to the back door in the kitchen. The front door was always locked three times since the night I got out by myself, but the kitchen door went right to the outside and was easier to unlock when I used the stool to get to the doorknob and the chain thing that Mom thought I wouldn't figure out. It was a little hard with the cast on one hand, but I figured it out with my good hand.

I walked down the sidewalk in a different direction this time so I could see Daddy without anyone bothering me. I still heard the sounds of the sidewalk people from down the street where the alleyway and the women wearing underwear were, but their voices got smaller and quieter behind me as I walked.

A car drove by slowly, and I saw a man with a big beard looking at me and shaking his head like I'd done something wrong. I decided I should be sneakier, so I walked in the shadows and hid behind different trees. I walked more and then crouched between parked cars.

I was wearing a blue shirt and my shorts that are like pants with straps that go over my shoulders and lots of pockets everywhere. There's a name for those kinds of pants, but I always forget what it is. I don't like describing clothes anyway.

The main thing is that I was wearing black shoes with Velcro so I didn't have to tie anything. I hated tying things. So did Tater. He always told me about the stuff he hated, so I tried to think of stuff I hated too. People think babies are always loving life and that they don't hate anything, but people are wrong about that. Babies hate stuff all the time. Tater told me that when we find stuff to hate it means we're becoming more like grown-ups. But Mom said that's a snobby way to think and that I have to look on the bright side more. So even though I hated things that have to be tied, it just meant I really loved buttons and snaps and Velcro a lot.

I found a good spot to see Daddy—right between a bus stop and a mailbox—and I pulled out my new bat and held it over my head with my good hand so it looked like it was flying.

"Daddy, look," I whispered.

I pressed on the bat to make it light up. It was almost the same color as Daddy.

"This is Ray," I said. "He's helping me."

I was surprised by my words and started to laugh. Like the other night in the alley with the green hair kid, my mouth was saying words I didn't know it could, and my laughter sounded really loud in the darkness, which made me laugh even more.

Daddy's face sparkled and his eyes looked down at me. "That's a beautiful bat you got there," he said. His voice sounded like it was meant only for me, like there was a tunnel going from his mouth to my ears. It sounded like it was wrapped in a blanket, and I got to hold it and unwrap it and touch the words. It sounded like Mom's voice but like a man's version of it. It sounded like a song you always remember, even when you can't recall where you first heard it.

It also sounded scary, like someone coming back to life. Like when you suddenly feel sick and throw up on yourself. Like when grown-ups cry because emotions are just so big on certain days. Even happiness could be frightening sometimes.

I didn't know what to say. The only other time I felt this way was when I met the Easter Bunny and all I could think about was how I wished he would live with me and Mom and paint eggs and eat chocolate with us all the time. But Mom said he only comes out of his rabbit hole on Easter, and I thought about how dark and sad it would be to live in a hole, and then someone took a photo of us right when I was crying, and that picture ended up on my bedroom wall.

But this wasn't the Easter Bunny. It was Daddy, and he was talking to me.

"What's your name?" he said.

This confused me because I thought he would know my name, but maybe he was really tired.

"Tony," I said. "Tony Volcano Ventura." I tried to hide my cast because I didn't want him to see it.

He made a sound like he was laughing, but it sounded more like big rocks rolling down a hill. His eyes brightened.

"I knew that," he said. "I was just checking. What do you want to call me?" he asked.

"Daddy," I said. My throat tightened after I said it, and I felt dizzy. I heard the big rock–rolling sound again.

"Take a deep breath, little Tony," he said.

I sat down on the ground and covered my face for a second but then got scared and looked up at him again. Everything around me—the trees, the stars, the streetlights, Daddy's face—looked blurry. I tried to stop the tears. I wanted to be strong.

"Do you like my hair?" He whispered like it was a secret thing he could only show me. I squinted up at him, trying to see his hair. "An asteroid did it," he said. If I listened closely, I could hear him breathing while he talked. I was happy that he was able to breathe up there.

"Somebody over there?" another voice called out. I hid behind the mailbox and peeked around it. The man with the big beard was looking around some bushes in front of an old house. He held a flashlight that kept blinking off and he had to hit it with his hand to make it come back on. I almost wanted to give him my light-up bat, but I was pretty sure he was looking for me.

"Here, baby, baby, baby," he sang quietly. Then I heard some meowing sounds, and a cat came out of the bushes and scared the man. He said a bad word and turned his flashlight off and walked back to his car.

I waited for him to drive off and then walked the other way. I looked up and saw Daddy's face, but I couldn't tell what his hair looked like or if he was playing a trick on me.

"Daddy, I'm over here now," I said. "Where do you want me to go?"

"Go to . . . ," he said, but his voice faded out.

I stopped to shine my bat light up at him. "What did you say, Daddy? Talk louder, please."

"The alley," he said. And then I heard a sound like a *whoosh whooooosh whoosh whooooop*, like a cartoon moon being squeezed by someone.

8

IT WAS AROUND this time when Mom told me a story about something that made her cry. She told me this when I was sad after dropping a Fruit Roll-Up in the street and getting dirt all over it. Her words calmed me down so much, like a soft pillow. She was talking to me in her grown-up voice, like she was talking to a grown-up. She wasn't reading to me out of a book or anything, but she was telling me a story. Some of it was hard to understand, but I listened to every word.

"One night," she said. "I woke up and realized we were all alone. You were only three months old, and I hadn't seen your dad since right after you were born. You were sleeping on a blanket next to my mattress on the floor. I put you there because I was scared of turning over in my sleep and hurting you somehow. I worried about so much right after you were born. I don't know if I was thinking straight. I didn't know if I would ever be in love again. I cried so hard that I had to get up and get a roll of toilet paper to clean up the tears and snot and slobber coming out of my face because when I thought about these moments, these parts of our future, I was sad that your dad might not be there. But then I thought about how connected you and I would be, how we'd be a team."

I thought about the word *team* and remembered when some guy at the mall asked me who my favorite football team was and I didn't really know what he meant. I made a burping sound, and he laughed and gave me a free sticker with a football helmet on it. The helmet had a bird on it. "That's your favorite team now," he said.

If mom and I were a team, I wondered what would be on our helmets.

"I know you're just a little goober today, but every day you'll become more of a man," she said. She squished my cheeks with both her hands and looked right into my eyes. "We can look at each other now and forget everything else in the world. Our eyes are mirrors. In three years it will be the same. And every year after that. Our eyes don't change. Our bodies change and our hair changes and the skin on our faces gets wrinkled, but our eyes are always the same."

She took her hands off my face, but I kept my eyes connected to hers and I realized I wasn't sad anymore. She waved her fingers in the air like they were sparklers.

"Everything around us will change." She pointed at her eyes and smiled. Then she pointed at my eyes and got serious again. "But this won't change. I'll take care of you, and you—believe it or not—will take care of me. I'm your mom. You're my son. We're not alone. When it comes down to it, we don't need anyone else."

And then she said I love you a bunch of times and I wanted to say it too, but I closed my eyes and fell asleep, holding one of her fingers so tight I could feel her heartbeat going through me.

9

I STOPPED in front of our apartment building and thought about going back inside. I reached into my bag and grabbed a purple-flavored juice box. I held it between my legs and poked the pointy end of the straw into the box with my good hand. I finally stuck it in and drank half the juice while looking down the street at the alleyway. Then up at Daddy. Then down the street again.

I walked toward the alley, wondering what Daddy wanted to show me there.

A man on the other side of the street saw me and ran over with his cell phone up to his face. "Hold on. I just found a lost baby," he said to someone on the phone.

I thought he was going to pick me up, but he froze there and watched me. I stopped walking too, so we both stood there, staring at each other and not moving. He was wearing a suit and tie, and his face looked smooth and clean, like the man who talked on the TV news. He seemed like he was trying to be motionless, like a statue, like we were playing Simon Says, but maybe he was scared of me.

"Simon says leave me alone," I tried to say, but it just sounded like I was sneezing. He slowly pushed some buttons on his phone and pointed it at me like he was taking a picture.

"Leave that baby alone!" I heard a woman say. "This ain't none of your business, boy!"

"Oh, sorry," the man said, looking around. "Is this your baby?"

"This is a neighborhood baby," she said. "So the answer is yes."

The man seemed unsure and didn't move.

The woman pulled something shiny and metal from her purse and said, "We take care of our own."

The man stepped back and put his phone away. "I hear you," he said. He walked away fast but turned around when he was farther down the street and yelled, "I was trying to help!"

"Go on!" the woman yelled back.

"I took a picture of him!" the man shouted.

"You can take a picture of my ass for all I care!" the woman said louder.

I waited for the woman to say something to me or pick me up, but she just looked at me and laughed. I started to run away, but she stepped in front of me and said, "Hold on now. Where you belong?"

I pointed toward the alleyway.

"Oh, you one of those kids from the Mexican restaurant? What's your name, baby?"

"Tony."

"Tommy?"

"Tony."

"Well, Tony, my name is Lanuola, but you can call me La-La. Let's take you back to the Mexican joint and see if your mom's done washing dishes or whatever."

She looked at my cast and frowned and then grabbed my other hand. We walked past the alley where Daddy wanted me to go and I tried to say something, but it sounded like I was

44

about to cry. I looked in the alley and thought I saw something move. La-La tightened her grip and told me not to fuss. She was wearing shoes that made her taller than my mom, and her shirt looked like one of those nets people catch fish in. Her pants were tight and red and made a squeaky sound when she walked.

She took me to a small Mexican restaurant with orange and yellow walls and dirty windows. There was one person sitting in a booth, eating something floppy with their hands, but half of whatever it was kept falling on the plastic tray he was hunched over. He laughed like it was a joke he was playing on himself. I almost laughed too.

The woman at the counter said, "Welcome to Banjo's. My name is Angela. May I take your order?" She looked down at me like she was trying to figure something out, but she had a bored look on her face.

"This baby belong to anyone here?" La-La asked.

Angela turned and shouted toward the kitchen, "Hector! You lose a baby?"

A young man came out of the kitchen. His white T-shirt was smeared with red splotches like he'd been in a fight. "It doesn't look like any of mine," he said.

"*Any* of yours?" Angela said. She gave him a weird look.

"I'm just kidding," he said. "I told you I'm a virgin."

"Yeah, like the blessed Mary, right?" she said back.

"This ain't nothing to joke about," La-La said. "The baby pointed to this place when I asked him what was up."

"Maybe he's hungry," Hector said. "I can make him a quesadilla if you want to call somebody."

I thought a quesadilla sounded pretty good, but I didn't know what to say. Mom had taught me to say "yes, sir" a few days before this. She said it was a big-kid thing I could say and that it meant something was serious.

"What's in his bag?" Angela said. "Any kind of ID or a note or something? Maybe his momma ran away. He's got a broken arm. Maybe his momma did that and then ghosted."

La-La rustled around in my bag like she was getting impatient. "Yeah, I doubt that," she said. She pulled Ray out, shook her head, and put him back. "Baby stuff," she said. Her eyes looked around for a clock and then frowned. "I better get some kind of reward for this." She looked at me and smiled through her bright red lips. I wanted to say, "Yes, sir," but I just smiled back.

When Hector brought out my quesadilla, he cut a piece for me, and its cheese stretched long like a rubber band. I chewed on a small square of it and the cheese stuck to my chin. That's when the door opened and a teenager in jeans and a basketball jersey said, "Oh, there he is." It was the same kid I saw in the alleyway on the first night I snuck out. He walked over to me like we were old friends. I guess maybe we were.

"You know this kid, Dylan?" La-La said.

"Yeah, yeah. He's my cousin."

La-La looked at him suspiciously and narrowed her eyes. I was kind of suspicious, too, because his hair was bright orange and not green like it was before. I thought maybe hair colors were like special codes. Doesn't orange mean caution, or does it just mean oranges?

"You're saying you know this baby?" La-la finally said.

"I am saying exactly that," he answered.

"Let me see your arms," she said to Dylan.

Hector cut another piece of the quesadilla for me and then cut a piece for himself. We were both chewing slowly as we watched La-La and Dylan talk about me.

Dylan's arms were partly covered in wristbands, and he moved them up and down between his wrist and elbow. "His dad's an astronaut," he said to La-La.

"Oh, really?" she said. "That's not a real job."

"Don't worry about it," he said. "I'll take care of him."

La-La pointed at one of his wristbands, a black and red one. "Why you got bruises on your left arm?"

"I fucked up a tattoo," he said.

"Watch your tongue," La-La said.

"We're closing up," Hector said. "One of you taking him home?"

"He lives over there," Dylan said, pointing somewhere through the window. "At Walnut Square. I got a key."

La-La made a groaning sound and said, "Well, tell his astronaut dad to put a tag on him or something. Letting your baby run around at night isn't right at all. He might break his other arm."

Dylan walked over to me, and even though I liked La-La, I was glad he was taking me home. Something about him made me feel more comfortable, like he was an older version of me or something. I wasn't sure how he knew where I lived, though. He cleared his throat and leaned over and tried to pick me up, but for some reason he couldn't do it right. It was as if he'd never held a baby before. He acted like I was really heavy, and everyone was watching him and looking worried as he tried to figure out where to put his arms under my legs. I said, "Down, please," and he finally gave up.

"Okay," he said, wiping sweat from his face. "You ready?"

I didn't know what to say. We both looked at the door and then slowly walked out together.

Once we were outside, Dylan laughed and shook his head. As we walked, he said, "I don't have a key, man. I hope you do. I wanted to get you away from that woman though. She's crazy."

"La-La?" I asked.

"Yeah. She'll be all sweet sometimes, but then she'll steal your shit and lie about it."

Just like the night I first saw Dylan in the alley, something different was happening inside my brain and I tried to talk.

"Let's go over here, please," I said, pointing to the alley.

Dylan looked at me, maybe surprised by my words or thinking I was playing a trick on him.

"Please, sir," I said.

For some reason, this made him laugh so hard that he was almost crying.

"I can't believe you called me 'sir,'" he said. "But I'm not really supposed to hang out there anymore. You know— because of the fuckin' pigs."

I'd heard that sometimes people kept pet pigs in the city and thought maybe that was why Daddy wanted me to go in the alley. Maybe he had a pet pig there and I could learn something about him that way.

"What's a fuckin' pig do?" I asked Dylan.

He laughed so loud and hard that it sounded like a cartoon laugh, like, *ha ha ha ha ha!* "You're too much, dude!" he said.

I walked toward the alley, but Dylan didn't move. I turned around and said, "C'mon, man." It was something I heard people say all the time when they wanted something.

"Okay, okay, okay," Dylan said. "You want to know what fuckin' pigs do?" He was serious now, whispering to me like he was telling me a secret. "They sneak up on babies and hit them with pipes. Then . . . then, they . . . um." He stopped and looked around. "They eat their faces."

My heart began to beat faster and I got confused, unsure why Daddy would want me to go to the alley if there were fuckin' pigs there that wanted to eat my face. I got scared and my face felt tingly.

"It's all right, man," Dylan said. He gave me a quick pat on my back. "It's something we all gotta learn in life. You should go home now. I know you live over there because I saw you and your mom once."

I pulled Ray out of my bag and squeezed him to make his bat body light up, but it scared Dylan too much and he made me put him away. We walked the rest of the way to my apartment building.

"I can go in the back door," I told him. "I know how to get in."

I was still mad about the pigs. I looked up to see if Daddy was in the sky. A gray cloud covered most of him, but I could see his eyes peeking over the top of it, like he was trying to hide. I shook my head, disappointed.

"Hey," Dylan said. "Did I get that part about your dad right? Like, he's an astronaut or something, right?"

"I don't know," I said. "I don't know what he is."

10

IN BED, UNDER my blankets with Ray, it felt like a dark cave. I squeezed him to make the dark light up and shook his body to make his wings flap. It was still nighttime outside, and I knew I should be sleeping but I couldn't stop imagining those pigs breaking into my room, looking for me. Maybe I could disguise myself so I didn't look like a baby they'd want to eat.

I unsqueezed Ray and let the dark come back all around me. I said "I'm not a baby" in the dark and got scared until I made Ray light up again. "Are you a baby bat?" I said, and I pressed him a bunch to make his light blink. I set him down on my chest and said, "Dark," into the blackness. I couldn't tell if I was turning on his light or if I was turning on the dark. I grabbed him quick and squeezed. It became a lit-up blanket cave. And then dark again. I had the power to make it either way.

A sound came from down the hall, the plastic click sound of a light switch. Someone was in the kitchen. The refrigerator door opened, and I heard Mom moving jars and food around. I didn't feel hungry because of the quesadilla, so I hoped it wasn't breakfast yet. As I listened for more sounds, I suddenly felt very tired. I stuck my head out of the blankets and pretended I was asleep in case she looked in my room. I heard the sound of bread disappearing into the toaster. It sounded like SHUNK! I waited for the air to smell different, and then it did, going from dry and boring to toasty and tan. It smelled like a warm hug.

"Do you want blueberry on yours?" Mom said to someone. I could tell she wasn't talking to me because she was in the other room and she was talking in a quiet voice.

I heard a muffled mumbling voice answer back. I listened as hard as I could to figure out whose voice it was. I pointed Ray at my door to see if he could hear anything. The door to my room wasn't closed all the way, and there was an inch of light on the floor. Even though he was lit up, I didn't think Ray could hear much either.

But then I heard a clearer voice say, "How is he lately?" It sounded like a man. Like a daddy.

"He's healthy," Mom said. "He's getting so smart."

I closed my eyes to listen better. Mom taught me that one night. Closing your eyes makes your smelling and your hearing better, she told me. I wondered if that was why she said I was getting smarter, because I could do tricks like that. With my eyes closed, I could almost picture them: Mom sitting in her favorite red chair, hunched forward, and the other person . . . I didn't know how to picture him. He was like a shadow, standing by the window. Maybe he looked like a superhero.

"Did you tell him about the fuckin' pigs?" he said.

I couldn't hear what she said back. I closed my eyes harder and got scared when I heard her say a word that sounded like "skeleton." The only thing I knew about skeletons was that they're made of bones and I had bones inside me but I couldn't really see them, and if I ever did see a bone sticking out of me, then that was a bad thing and I had to put it back in before I died.

Then I heard a scratching sound outside my window. I looked over and saw a face. It looked like a mask, but its mouth was moving and it was breathing really hard and making the glass foggy. I pointed Ray's light at the window and could see

51

that it was Dylan. He called my name but it sounded weird, like he was changing his voice. He sounded like an old man. I looked closer and saw that his hair suddenly looked white. I didn't know how it could change so fast. First it was green, then orange, then white. I wished it was brown, like mine.

"Come out here," he said. "Have some."

He was chewing on something.

"What?" I said. "What is it?"

"It's the best part," Dylan said. His hand busted through the window and he was holding some kind of small leg. Blood ran down his fingers, and I couldn't tell if it was coming from him or the leg. Two of the toes were chewed off, and I could hear crying baby sounds coming from somewhere. Dylan snorted and laughed louder than the baby sounds, and his face had that flat kind of pig nose wiggling between his eyes. His hand with the leg came at me and I stopped breathing for a second, and then I was yelling as loud as I could.

Mom was there quickly and picked me up. "What's wrong, sweetie?" she said. "It's okay now. Mommy's here."

I looked at the window, and my face reflected back at me, unbroken. There was no blood anywhere. No white-haired Dylan or pig. No leg. The sun was out, and I heard the sounds of kids playing. I smelled toast coming from our kitchen, and Mom asked me, "Do you want blueberry?"

I kept looking at the window while trying to breathe normally. I'm not sure I wanted to eat anything right then.

"Baby baby blueberry," Mom sang in my ear. She seemed to be in a good mood. She sang so sweetly, "Baby baby blueberry . . . baby berry blue . . . this is how I love you." She made up songs all the time. She always rhymed *blue* with *you*. I liked it.

I began to feel awake and calm. My arms stretched up and I yawned. But then she stopped singing, and I heard a baby crying somewhere outside.

11

I COULDN'T STOP eating the toast. Mom had smeared blueberry jelly on it, and I ate so much she had to make more. As she was making scrambled eggs, a man came out of her room and sat at the table by my tall chair. His hair was sticking up high on one side like the wind had blown hard against that part of his head. He smelled strange, kind of like a bus. It took me a second to realize it was Ben.

"Say good morning to Ben," Mom said. "We're going to have a short meeting before work today, sweetheart."

She gave him a cup of coffee, and he smiled at me in that way grown-ups sometimes do when they're fake-smiling at a camera. He reminded me of oatmeal.

"Happy Fourth of July!" he said. He took a sip of his coffee, but he was still smiling and it spilled a little down his chin. He seemed nervous and weird, and his white T-shirt had small brown stains on it.

"We're all going to watch the fireworks on the river tonight," Mom announced. "You didn't like it last year, but you had an ear infection, so that's probably why. This year will be more fun. Tater's coming too."

When Mom and Ben dropped me off at Tater's for the afternoon, they talked more about the fireworks and how excited they were to see them. Tater's mom and dad were coming too. Tater thought it meant something serious about Ben.

"If my mom and dad are there and your mom is there with a man, I think it's like a wedding," he said.

I tried to repeat the word. "Weddy?"

"It's when a guy gets on his knees and kisses a woman's hand and then he's your new dad. And then the fireworks go off in the sky and everyone cheers."

"New dad?" I said.

"Well, I think so," he said. "Usually my mom and dad only go out with other moms and dads. So Ben will probably be your dad."

I didn't know what to think of this. My head felt like the blanket cave when it went from light to dark, and my chest hurt. Tater must have sensed my confusion because he put his arm around me.

"It's okay," he said. "Ben is cool. He gave me a toy train once. It didn't work, but it was my favorite color."

I tried to understand the whole new dad thing. What happened to my old dad?

"Do you want to know what my favorite color is?" Tater asked. "It's silver."

That night, me and Mom and Ben and Tater and his mom and dad spread out a giant blanket on the grass by the river and ate potato chips and hot dogs while everyone around us drank beer and kept looking at the sky like they were waiting for something. I saw little kids running around with sparkly sticks. Some of the bigger kids threw these little balls at each other, and then a bunch of green and red smoke came out of the balls and it smelled really bad. A lot of girls screamed when the balls got close to them, like it was poison smoke.

Daddy was high up over the river, and as the sky got darker, his face became brighter. He was shiny blue and smiling, reflecting a silver spot on the water below him. I started to feel sleepy as I watched him, wondering if he'd talk to me with all the other people around. I saw his face move a little, like he was winking. I thought he was trying to send me messages. I had Ray with me, and I made his wings blink for Daddy to see. A couple of kids ran over to me and asked about Ray. They thought he was a firework, but when they found out he wasn't, they acted bored and ran away to look for more sparkly or smoky things.

Mom watched me and smiled, like she knew I was communicating with Daddy. I kept worrying that Ben was going to kiss her hands and become my new dad, but they just sat close to each other not doing much. Sometimes Ben put his hand on Mom's back or her knee. I wanted to run over and make him stop touching her. I wanted to point to my glowing Daddy and show Ben who my real dad was, the dad who was always there, even when he was on the other side of the world.

Suddenly I heard a whistling sound, and everyone turned quiet and looked to the sky. A bunch of popping sounds got louder and faster, like *pop-pop-pop-pop-pop!* A red, white, and blue flower of light appeared in the sky, right under Daddy's face, and everyone cheered. I looked at Mom and she could tell I was worried.

"Those are the fireworks, honey," she said. Her voice had a jump in it, like she needed to talk fast and loud to match the popping. "Look at the pretty fireworks. Look at the colors! Watch!"

But what about Daddy? I thought. As the fireworks continued, they drifted a little more away from his face, like maybe he was blowing them away or maybe he was floating farther away. The fireworks became bigger and more complicated and music played from somewhere. Maybe an orchestra was playing on one of the boats in the river. Maybe it was the wedding music. I looked at Ben, but he just squinted and burped as he watched the fireworks explode all over each other. Some of the fireworks looked like they were coming out of the other fireworks. They popped higher and higher like a ladder of lights. Daddy looked happy, his face changing colors. Some of the fireworks danced fast and bright, and some of them sparked and spread out like slow-motion lightning. The music and lights sped up as the people cheered more and more, and I even heard other kids saying, "Wow!" and "Oh my God!" I wondered if Daddy was watching all of us and if the fireworks scared him at all. They started happening faster, and soon there were three or four explosion flowers happening at the same time, and the music got more serious with lots of clanging and tooting and *boom boo-boo-boom!* I saw some of the sparks getting close to Daddy and wondered if he could feel them.

I turned to look at Mom and saw her and Ben kissing and laughing. I didn't know if they were wedding kisses, but my body turned hot like an angry firework. I ran to them to break it up but tripped over Mom's purse on the blanket and fell. I managed to roll my body in time so I wouldn't land on my cast, but it still hurt, and I cried out. Mom rushed over and picked me up, asking me if I was okay. I noticed Ben at that moment with an angry look on his face—the kind of look a baby gets when you take his binky away.

"Daddy up there," I said. "Daddy say no boom! Daddy say no boom!"

Everyone around us was cheering the fireworks and she couldn't understand what I was trying to say. The fireworks stopped right after that and the sky became a whistling sound around us and all the other people in the dark. Smoke floated through the sky in front of Daddy's face and I could see he was watching me.

"No new daddy," I said. "No kiss hands."

Mom kissed my hands. "Oh!" she said.

I noticed Ben opening a can of beer as she did this. He held it against his mouth. I was watching him through blurry tears.

"Oh," Mom said again. My hands were damp and slippery on her face and chin. "Oh, your poor hands," she said.

I looked around to see if anyone else was noticing my sadness. I saw the shadow of someone throwing up near the water and the sound of splashing and excited voices mixed together. People walked back to their cars or their homes, blankets, baskets, and babies bundled in their arms. Maybe it was over. Maybe I broke up the kissing just in time. I looked at Tater between his mom and dad, holding their hands. They looked worried about me.

"Hey, Tony," Tater shouted. "That was pretty cool, right?"

12

I WAS AT THE PARK with Mom and Tater, but I wasn't supposed to climb on things because of my cast. It was Mom's day off from work and she was watching us both. A lot of times when Tater and I were together, she'd read a book or a magazine and let us do whatever we wanted. We played in the sand pit and I was getting sand in my cast, but it felt kind of good because my arm had been itchy forever. Mom said she'd help me clean it out later with a vacuum and straw. I thought she was joking at first, but she was actually serious. I took my pants off in the sand pit because it was hot outside. I was wearing big-boy Pull-Ups anyway, and they're exactly like shorts. Tater said sometimes grown-ups wear Pull-Ups too.

"You know what's yummy?" Tater said. He wrestled something out of the pocket of his shorts. I watched and waited without saying anything because one time he asked me that and I said, "Eggs," and he got really mad and said, "No! M&Ms!" and then wouldn't give me any.

A big plastic bag of something flopped out of his pocket and onto a sand pile between us. It looked too big to fit in his pocket and it was full of burnt pieces of bacon.

"Beef jerky, buddy!" he said.

I touched the bag and said, "Bacon?" I was confused and

feeling it through the plastic to see if it was real. Maybe it was toy bacon.

"No, it's different from bacon. It's chewy and delicious. One hundred percent jerky, buddy."

I wasn't sure why he kept calling me "buddy," but I was curious to try whatever it was. He moved it out of my reach and then dug a hole in the sand. "Let's bury it first. Then we'll dig it up and pretend it's our only food." Tater was extra excited about this, so I let him make up this new game.

I helped him dig the hole bigger and we were laughing a lot. "Hundred cent, buddy," I said.

"Yeah, yeah, we're digging a grave," Tater said. "And then, and then—we'll be zombies!" But he said it like "zooooombies."

I wasn't sure what a zombie really was because I was too young to watch shows with scary teeth and blood in them. I thought zombies were people who were dead or almost dead or just really slow and tired and their clothes were always torn up, so they probably tripped over them all the time. They didn't seem scary to me, but I knew Tater would probably teach me about why they were.

Tater made sure the bag was closed so the jerky stayed protected and then put it in the hole. We pushed a bunch of sand over it and patted it down, and then Tater took his army guy action figure and set him on top to mark it.

Mom looked over at us and asked if we wanted a snack, but Tater called out before I could and said, "No thanks!" Behind her, I saw a rat run quickly into a bush. I worried that the rat would get our snacks and also that it might scare Mom or try to attack her.

"Mom!" I yelled. I stood up and walked faster toward her, closely watching the bush behind her, careful of the rat.

"Hey, what about the jerky?" Tater said as Mom handed

me a tangerine. I turned around and saw him running around the sand pit like he was trying to start a sand tornado. He fell down and yelled to the blue sky, "I am a sad zombie!"

I ate the tangerine in quick, messy bites, juice squirting on my arm and running down my chin. I concentrated on the bush in case the rat tried to come out. Maybe I would give it a piece of bread, but if it was a mean rat, I'd smash it with my cast.

Some guy with gray hair and glasses walked over to us and said, "That orange looks delicious." He winked at me, or maybe at Mom. He reminded me of a grandpa. His skin was tan-colored with grandpa spots. I tried to stay focused on where the rat was hiding. I heard Tater groaning in the sand pit.

"I'm making zombie sounds," he said. "Come back and save me!"

I saw the rat's head suddenly poke out of the bush. I jumped back and bonked into the old guy's legs. The rat flew out of the bush and flipped in the air like a daredevil, somersaulting like an animal in the circus. It landed in the middle of us and the guy did a quick dance and let out a funny sound. I threw the rest of my tangerine at the rat and hit it in the butt as it ran away. The rat didn't know where it was going and stopped for a second, and then scampered back to the clump of tangerine to sniff it. Tater shouted, "Wild animal!" and came out of the sand box, wobbling like a zombie with his arms out in front of him.

Mom grabbed me and lifted me off the ground, both arms wrapped around me for protection. She called out to Tater, "Don't get near it!" The rat snatched the tangerine piece and ran away to the other side of the park. There were other kids over there and every few seconds a different one screamed.

"You were very brave," Mom said, kissing the top of my head. I didn't really feel brave, but I did feel like a cat probably feels when it gets puffed up to scare something. I once saw a cat hissing at a dog and its fur blew up like a big cloud all over its head. My head probably looked like that—an angry cat wearing a fur coat.

The man was still standing near us and laughing like he'd heard a good joke. "That was one scary rat," he said.

Mom gave him a funny look. "And who are you again?" she asked.

"Oh, I'm Chad," he said, brushing off his pants like he had rat germs on them. He held out his hand. Mom looked at it for a second, like she was counting his fingers before she shook it.

"I'm Jennie," she said back to him as their hands went up and down like a seesaw.

"I was going to offer you some jackfruit," he said. He opened a bag and pulled out a plastic bowl with a lid on it. "It's sweet and delicious. Have you ever had it?"

Mom looked into the plastic bowl as he took the lid off. She made a grimace and said, "Yeah, we've had that," but I don't think she was telling the truth.

I tried to see what it looked like. "Jack foot," I said. It smelled good.

"Okay, just one piece," Mom said. "Is it fresh?" she asked the Chad man.

"I only buy it in the can. That way you don't have to take out the seeds. It's hard to get it fresh here," he said. He took out a couple of plastic forks and stabbed some pieces for us. I thought it was cool that he had a lot of plastic forks in his bag. Tater ran over, and the man looked surprised. "Another one?" he said.

"Are you sharing treats?" Tater said.

We all stood there, taking small bites of the strange fruit. It tasted like pineapple to me, but not as sour.

"It's the national fruit of Bangladesh," the Chad man said.

"I like Banglabash," Tater said.

Chad man laughed and then said to Mom, "Where's the dad of these guys?"

Mom made another funny face and then tried to smooth it out. She patted Tater on the head. "Well, this one belongs to a friend, and his dad is probably working." Tater made loud slurpy sounds as he chewed on his piece of jackfruit.

There was a quiet moment, only the sounds of other kids and some birds in the air, as I waited to hear Mom talk about Daddy. The Chad man looked like he was waiting too. He sort of leaned in with his ears and made a sound like *mm-hmm*.

"Daddy," I said, pointing up.

"Oh," he said as if he was figuring something out.

"Yeah," Mom said. She got kind of quiet, maybe so I couldn't hear her. "He's out there somewhere," she said, making it sound top secret.

"I'm sorry," he said, holding out the bowl to offer more jackfruit to her. I wondered how many other people he gave fruit to. I wondered if he walked around every day, giving out different fruits. Maybe he'd have watermelon next time.

"It's personal," Mom said. "I mean, nothing personal."

I didn't know what she meant by that. Was she saying Daddy was some kind of nothing person? I thought the moon was a person because I heard it talk and say it was my Daddy. Maybe a nothing person was one that couldn't touch or hold you but could still talk. If a mountain with a face could talk, or even a dog or phone or statue in a church, is that what "nothing personal" meant? I'd seen people talk to those things before. I even saw someone talk to the waffles in the freezer at the grocery store once. I was pretty sure people didn't always have human bodies. Sometimes they were just stories with lots of words.

"Well, thank you for the fruit, Chad," Mom said. "We have to get going."

Tater ran over to the sand pit and dug up his one hundred percent jerky. We climbed into the backseat of the car and got buckled in. Tater was bigger than I was so his chair was more of a booster and mine was like a clunky throne with a giant pillow that held me in place. I looked at the Chad guy as we drove off, and he just stood there, looking up in the sky with a sad look and his bag of fruit. Maybe he would look for my dad too, I thought. But right when I thought that, I knew he probably wouldn't know how to. I sniffled, and Mom looked in the mirror. I tried to stay tough and strong, but a tear came out and she asked me what was wrong.

"Nothing personal," I tried to say.

"No thing person."

13

SOMETIMES if I slept through the whole night, I'd wake up early, before Mom, and patiently wait for her to wake up too. But if I was hungry, I'd yell from my bed until she came and got me. If that didn't work, I'd get out of bed and stand by her bedroom and make beeping alarm sounds until her arms woke up and moved around, feeling for her clock. She'd push a button and I'd get quiet for a minute and then start making sounds again. When she hit her clock, I'd stop beeping again. The rest of her body didn't move. Her arm was like a sleepy sock puppet.

When her real alarm did go off, she'd say, "Damn snooze button," or "Snooze button, will you do what I say?" I used to think she was saying "smooth button," and I looked at her clock to see which button was the smooth one. There was more than one smooth button. What if she hit the wrong one? I guess when you grow up your arms and hands just know where to go.

Sometimes when I wasn't hungry in the morning, I'd get out of bed and wander around the apartment. I liked to sit in the empty bathtub with a car and a boat and an airplane and make them race against each other.

One time I tried to turn on the TV, but I couldn't figure out how it worked, so I looked at the black screen and saw my shape looking back at me. It was so quiet that I got scared for a second and looked out the window to make sure the world was okay. I saw some tree branches waving around. Mom had told me Daddy blows kisses to us at night sometimes to show he loves us. I thought Daddy might be blowing kisses for those trees too, even as the sun was coming up. Sitting on one of the branches was a small blue bird, but it wasn't moving or making a sound. I watched it, waiting for something. Maybe it was sleeping like everyone else. It didn't move for a long time and I wondered if it wanted me to go outside so it could tell me something. Maybe it had a message.

I wanted to tell Mom about the bird and the tree and something blowing through it. I walked to her room and slipped through the door without moving it. I wondered if her wake-up alarm was going to go off. She was quiet, and I couldn't tell if she was breathing. I watched her hand that wasn't tucked in her blanket to see if it would move. I made my own alarm sound but softer than usual and only one time. I decided to not wake her up, so I sat on her floor and thought about the bird outside. I told myself that if it were still there later, that meant it had a message for me. Or maybe it was watching over me, or us.

As I was about to fall back asleep, Mom woke up without the alarm going off. She stretched and yawned and made her legs shake in a funny way.

"Well, hey, early bird," she said to me.

I liked how quiet it was in the morning, like everybody's life had all the time in the world. Like happiness was all around us, even if we didn't realize it. Sometimes in books and on TV they'd say, "To be continued," and I knew mornings could be like that, too—to be continued.

When I looked out the window later, the blue bird was gone. But there was a red bird sitting on the branch where it had been, not moving at all. And then later a yellow bird was there. It looked like a statue. I watched it to see if it would do something, but when I tapped on the window, it still didn't move. It looked like it was watching something, but I couldn't tell what it was looking at. The bird's eyes looked so small.

I went to grab Ray so I could show him the bird. I thought since he was a bat, maybe they were family. When I got back to the window, the yellow bird wasn't there. Instead, it was a black bird, and it was looking right at us.

14

THE BONES in my arm grew back together. Mom said I could have it cut off, and I think she meant my cast but I wasn't sure as we drove to the doctor's place. I imagined life with one arm. Maybe if you broke your arm and you weren't all the way grown up, then you can't get it fixed. Maybe if I broke it when I was old it would be different. Maybe it would have been okay to break because it wasn't as new. All the parts of my body were pretty new, I guess. If I broke my legs or my toes, maybe they'd stop growing and I'd walk with a limp like Dylan did when he walked me home that night. I thought of Dylan and wondered how many broken bones he'd had in his life. If you told me he had broken every bone in his body, I would have believed you because he did look sort of broken up inside. I wondered if they put casts on the insides of people.

At the doctor's office, a man who didn't look like a doctor but said he was a doctor was smiling big and holding something behind his back. I knew it was probably something sharp and scary, and I felt afraid. I told myself to never ever jump through a wall of blocks again. I would never break out of jail or even pretend to break out of jail ever again.

"I'm Dr. Fuller," the man said. "Are you ready to get this annoying lump off you?"

I wished he were Dr. Duck-Duck. I liked her better. I

didn't know how to answer his question. It sounded like a trick.

"This won't hurt at all," he said. "It might tickle, though."

I noticed the saw in his hand then, and it sort of looked like a toy.

"This is a special tool," he explained. "It doesn't cut. It vibrates like magic. It can't harm you." He tapped it against his chest. "Almost feels like a massage," he said, and laughed.

I kept looking at his chest as he said something else to Mom. I was waiting for his blood to start pouring out, but maybe he was a robot. It would make sense. I'd heard people on the street say there were robots everywhere pretending to be people.

Mom hugged me from the side and said this was a big, brave moment for me. It didn't feel like a normal hug, though. It felt like she was holding me still, like she had to do the first time I got my hair cut. I remember how I'd thought it was going to hurt, like my hair had feelings. But in the end, it only hurt a little and my hair grew back and kept growing after that. Maybe things that grow don't stay hurt forever.

But what about my arm?

The doctor explained, finally, that the saw wouldn't touch my skin and it shouldn't hurt, but if it did sting or feel weird, then I should raise my other hand. He turned on his little saw and it began buzzing really loud. My body shriveled up like a turtle trying to vanish into its shell. The shiny wheel touched the pink cast, and when I realized it wasn't going to stab into my skin, I untensed myself and watched as the doctor made little cuts into the cast. He cut a line down one side and then the other. He hummed a song while doing this, but the saw was so loud I couldn't hear what it was at first. When he turned it off, I heard him singing the alphabet, forward and backwards. I tried to follow along to make sure he was getting it right. I knew the alphabet all the way to *F*. It sounded like there were a million letters I hadn't learned yet, the way his song kept going.

I was so stuck on the doctor's alphabet song that I didn't even pay attention to the nurse who came in and used another tool on my cast to loosen it from my arm. When I looked down at the tool, I saw the cast was so loose that it finally slid off. It was a smelly pink shell. The doctor asked me to slowly make a fist and move my wrist. It seemed to work. My arm was alive.

I learned something about myself that day, but I wasn't sure exactly what. Maybe that I belonged in one piece, or that I could be healed from anything.

Before we left, the nurse showed me a big box of toys I could choose something from. I grabbed a sparkly necklace thing. But the necklace was connected to a leash, and for some reason the leash was like a bendy rope.

"Oh, this is a cute one!" the nurse said. She showed me how to hold the leash so the sparkly necklace wasn't touching the ground. "Invisible puppy," she said.

I'm not sure I understood, but she walked around with it, and it did look like she was walking an invisible dog. She made a barking sound and I smiled. I held the leash with my new unbroken arm and looked at the floating necklace.

Mom said, "That's a pretty collar. What's your dog's name?"

I didn't want it to be a collar. I wanted it to be a super-power necklace.

Mom bent down and pretended to pet the dog that wasn't there. I wondered what had happened to the dog—how it got away, if it was really invisible, and what I would feed it. Could I be one of those people who takes their dog everywhere? Would it scare pigs away?

15

ME AND MOM and Ben were at the mall, eating pretzels with cheese sauce on them. It had been a few days since I'd gotten my cast off, and my arm was finally not itchy and crusty anymore. Mom had been putting stuff that looked like cake frosting on it, but she said I wasn't supposed to lick it off. The pretzel was a reward for surviving a broken arm. I didn't really like pretzels much, though, unless the cheese sauce was really cheesy. I'd rather have cheese by itself.

I wasn't sure why Ben got a pretzel. I don't think he'd fractured anything. I don't even think I'd ever seen a Band-Aid on him. I watched him hogging all the cheese sauce and I was getting more and more mad. He also smelled funny that day. I heard Mom ask him what the smell was, and Ben said the name of some cologne that was in a different language, and Mom said, "Oh, you so fancy today!" and I coughed because whatever it was made me feel like I couldn't breathe like normal.

I wanted Daddy to walk up and punch Ben in the nose and slap the pretzel out of his hand and take me to Hickory Farms for cheese instead. I was still a little mad at Daddy, too, for trying to trick me about the alleyway and the fuckin' pigs, but I was starting to think maybe I was supposed to go and fight the pigs so they wouldn't eat other babies' faces. Maybe I had to become a hero to make Daddy return.

But how do you kill a pig? Do you push their face in more than it's already pushed in? Do I trick it to fall in a hole so it can't climb out? Was I supposed to grab them by their pig legs and spin them around and around until they got too dizzy and died? Do pigs get dizzy? Do pigs have sharp pig teeth? Is that how they'd eat my face? Do pigs smile and make gross sounds because their noses are ugly? I touched my nose to make sure it wasn't ugly. It felt okay. It didn't feel like a butt, which is what I thought a pig nose would feel like.

Ben was laughing at something and snorting like a pig. He held up a pretzel and said, "I was just thinking, if you keep breaking your arm, it would probably look like this pretzel."

Mom told him to shut his trap, but that made him laugh more, like he'd gotten away with something sneaky. I didn't understand half the stuff he said anyway. He was worse than a baby. More like a pig—kind of dumb and rubbery and making fart sounds. His mouth moved like a piggy mouth and his tongue looked kind of slimy, like a lollipop that fell out of a baby's mouth and landed in the dirt. I didn't know how Mom could stand him.

"Let's go down to the jewelry store," Ben said. His fingers were touching Mom's fingers and he was grinning really big.

Mom moved her hand away from his and said, "Is that why you got all cleaned up today? You trying to impress someone?"

"I'm trying to impress *you*," he said. "I mean, I'm simply being decent. I know how much that means to you."

"Don't get any big ideas," Mom said.

We ate the rest of our pretzels and started walking. Mom picked me up and groaned because I weighed more than a sack of potatoes, she said. I didn't know what they had at the jewelry store, but I got the feeling it was serious grown-up stuff because everyone was so quiet there. One guy who looked like a police officer watched everyone like they weren't allowed to have fun. I got bored because they didn't have anything for kids. As we looked at all the sparkly rings and necklaces in the glass cases, a couple of the workers looked at me like I was some kind of dangerous criminal. I don't know what their problem was, so I took my sunglasses out and put them on, but that didn't seem to calm them down. A tall red-haired man in a suit asked Ben if he was looking for "something special," and then he looked at me like he was confused. He tried to smile, but I could tell he wasn't good at smiling.

"Seeing what you got," Ben said, and the man nodded and frowned but then tried to smile again. He just couldn't do it.

I felt sad for him, so I smiled and said, "Shiny here." I'm not sure why I said it, but it made the man smile for real. The police guy twitched his face at me like that was all I was allowed to say, like he was sending me a message with his eyes that said, "Be quiet."

"You got that right, Tony." Ben said it like we were buddies. "Sometimes these cubic zirconia really sparkle."

One of the other salesmen talked really fast at Ben, as if he had said something wrong. "Sir, you're looking at certified real diamonds," he said. "But if you are looking for something more affordable, we do have diamond alternatives in this other sales case."

Ben's eyes blinked a lot, like somebody had thrown water in his face and he looked confused and suddenly angry. Mom laughed and said something about getting a ring from the gumball machines. I wanted to go look at the gumball machines. I got a ring from one once and it had a cool green star, but Mom took it away from me because I kept putting it in my mouth. The green star one tasted okay, but I wanted one with a red star instead. I would only put it in my mouth when Mom wasn't looking, I thought. That way I could keep it forever. I knew that rings were important for some reason, even though pants and shirts were usually more noticeable.

"You don't think I'm serious," Ben said to Mom. He looked at me for a second like I might know a lot about rings, and then he looked at the salesman. "How much is this one?" he asked, pointing at a really complicated one that looked like it wouldn't feel good in my mouth.

The salesman took his time to answer, almost like he didn't really want to. "That one is $9,650, sir."

I heard Ben fart a little and make a funny coughing sound. He stared at the salesman but didn't say anything. It looked like he might start crying.

"Okay," he said. "Well, okay. Okay, then." He told Mom to take me to the gumball machines so he could talk to "the nice gentleman" for a few minutes. But he said "gumball machines" and "nice gentleman" like he really hated those words.

"What a sad man," Mom said as we walked through the mall. It made me wonder if Daddy was a sad man too. I knew he wasn't like other dads because he wasn't around like other dads. But was he not here because he was sad, or was he sad because he wasn't here? All around the mall were pictures of families with moms and dads and kids, and they all looked happy, not sad. What if my dad was like the dads in those pictures? Would he be like a man who always smiled and had nice hair and muscles that aren't too big or too small? Would he tell good jokes and then laugh up at the sun? Would he make perfect hot dogs on a new outdoor grill, wearing an adult bib? I saw some guys at the mall who may have actually been real dads, but not many. They walked with their kids and held their hands. I didn't know what a dad hand felt like. Maybe like a mom hand, I guessed, with more dirt and hair. Some of the dads who were walking—the hand-holding dads—did look sad, though. They wore little shorts and ugly socks and weird sandals and sounded tired when they talked. I couldn't imagine Daddy in those clothes, especially the sandals. He would wear really cool shoes, like the kind astronauts wear.

Maybe he was going to be the moon forever. I thought about going there when I grew up. It didn't look very big.

At the gumball machines, I was excited about the one with tiny rings in it. I pointed at a ring with a red heart that I wanted, and Mom found some money to put in the slot. But we didn't get the red one. We got one with an American flag on it. Mom put in more quarters, and we kept getting the wrong one. Would she possibly spend $9,650 trying to get this special ring? When we finally did get the red heart one, Mom put it on my thumb and kissed me. I felt really happy in that moment, like it was the best day of my life ever.

"Now you're my son *and* my husband," she said, laughing really hard. I laughed, too, and then Ben walked up. He looked like a sad mall dad, but not *my* dad.

Mom held my hand, but not Ben's.

16

I WAS HELPING Mom make a poster at Crown Thrift. It was for a back-to-school sale, and I was picking out the colors of the markers. I was also coloring in a coloring book I'd found in that morning's donations. It was full of pictures of different kinds of superheroes and villains. Some of them were already colored in so perfectly that they looked real. I'd guess it was a teenager who had colored them. I tried to make my coloring as neat as theirs, but it looked sloppy, like a tornado. Some of my markers were worn out, so I had to use some broken crayons too. I liked them better. I thought maybe it wasn't a kid who'd finished some of the pages after all. Maybe it was a grown-up. That would make sense. Their pictures were made with bright markers that were not worn out. Grown-ups always want things to look neat and pretty.

I was coloring in a turtle with a gold crayon. Mom said she liked it. We were in the part of the store where they sold tables and chairs and dressers and even a piano. Sometimes people sat at the piano and played songs. I remember the first time someone played a song on it and it scared me because I'd thought it was a table. I didn't know that some tables were also things that made music. There was a sign by the piano that said No Billy Joel, and I got sad for Billy Joel because he wasn't allowed to play it. Mom even said to a customer once, "No

Billy Joel in this store," and I wondered why Billy Joel wasn't allowed at Crown Thrift and what he did to get into such trouble. For some reason, I imagined him with a hook for a hand and long hair. Maybe he stole pianos.

A woman walked into the store and said hi to Mom like they were old friends. They even hugged. The woman had a boy with her. He was wearing a bow tie and playing some kind of game that chirped in his hand. Her name was Energy and the boy's name was Exley. I'd never heard of people with names like those, and they both seemed strange, like they were from a TV show or something. Energy was wearing a shirt that only covered her chest, and a bunch of her skin was naked. I stopped coloring and looked at her arms and shoulders and her belly button. I thought about what was inside her belly button and what it was for. Did it move or do anything that my belly button couldn't do? For some reason I wanted to put my mouth on it. I looked at Exley then and he gave me a little smile and a nod. I thought he must be school age because he seemed smart and was taller than the piano. His clothes made him look like a grown-up. I wondered if he ever put his mouth on his mom's belly button. I think that's when I realized that babies came out of belly buttons, but hers seemed so small.

Mom and Energy talked while Exley looked at my coloring book with me and told me I was good at choosing the colors. He told me he'd had a gold turtle once, and then I pictured a sparkling turtle wearing a bow tie. It made me feel good that Exley was looking through the coloring book, and I imagined that was what having a big brother felt like. When he saw the pages with the super neat expert coloring on them, he said my turtle was better. He pointed at a man on the next page with big muscles and giant wings coming out of his back and said I should color that next.

"Wing man," I said.

"Yeah, that's a good name," he said.

I heard Mom laugh at something Energy was saying, and they both took a few steps away from us like they were trying to sneak away. I wanted to hear what was so funny and I tried to watch them as Exley started playing his game again. When Energy smiled, she looked like happy sunshine and her face somehow got bigger, and even though I had to go to the bathroom, I could feel my face doing what her face was doing, or maybe I was trying to make her face do what mine was doing. I wanted to hear her laugh and see if her body got shaky and funny like Mom's does sometimes.

I looked down and saw that my hand had dragged a red crayon over the big-muscled wing man. It looked like someone had smeared him with lipstick. When I looked up at Energy again, she looked right at me but with sort of a sad look. I felt embarrassed about my coloring book and about my sloppy wing man. Mom looked serious and said something low and whispery to Energy. I heard her say the words "even though that was a long time ago." Energy looked at Mom and then toward me again. It was like she was looking at me and Exley and seeing us for the first time. It seemed like she was thinking about her life and not feeling good about it.

"You never really loved him," I heard Energy say. "You were mean to him." I saw Mom grab Energy's hand and then move a little more away from us. I couldn't tell if Mom's hand was being nice or being hard. She looked tired, like she suddenly had a headache.

Exley leaned down to me and said quietly, "I think she's talking about Daddy. She's always mad about Daddy."

"Daddy," I said.

"Where's your daddy?" Exley asked.

"Upstairs," I said, though I'm not sure why. I had never said the word *upstairs* before, and now I imagined going up the stairs to the office and finding the moon there, floating, by the time clock. I was surprised by my mouth and my growing list of words. I wanted to say it loud so Mom would hear me and add it to her notebook. Then I said, "Downstairs."

"Oh!" Exley said. "Let's pretend upstairs is Heaven and downstairs is heck and see what your daddy's doing."

I'd heard of heck, but Mom called it hell. It was the place we went when she had to wait in line and mail presents to someone. One time it was the place we went to get her driver's license.

"Hellllll," I said. I made the word sound like Mom makes it sound when she was angry and moaning.

"Tony!" Mom said. "That's not nice."

"We were playing a game," Exley said. "We were going to look for his daddy."

"Were you really?" Mom said.

"It's probably time for us to go," Energy said. She took Exley's hand and I watched them walk toward the door. Energy's back was so smooth, and it looked like she was dancing, the way she walked. I wanted her to turn around so I could see her face again. I wanted to see what it looked like sideways. Sunshine or moon?

"Bye-bye," I called out to them, but they didn't answer. Energy paused at the door like she'd forgotten something, her hand the Push sign. "Bye-bye," I said again, and she turned back to me. Her face was sun and moon both.

"Be good to your mom," she said.

There was a hanging bell by the top of the door that rang when people came in and out of the store. Sometimes it seemed so loud and sometimes I didn't even hear it. I couldn't figure out who could have put it up there. When Energy and Exley left, the music of the bell shook and stayed in the air. I looked at the coloring in my book again and Mom was quiet for a long time. I didn't even notice the bell the rest of the day, but I tried to make the sound of it with my mouth. It was stuck in my head like a sad song.

17

THE STREET SMELLED funny that night—part poop and part flowers. Part of it was also that jelly stuff Mom rubbed on my chest when she wanted me to stop coughing. I was standing in front of a big window down the street from home. I was close enough to the alley that I could have run in there and hid from someone if they saw me. But I was still kind of scared of the pigs and Daddy hadn't said anything else to me since the night he tried to trick me into the alley. I'd snuck out two other times to talk to him since then, but he didn't say anything, so I just went home.

I didn't even try to find La-La or Dylan, but I knew they were probably wandering around somewhere in the neighborhood. I couldn't imagine them anywhere else.

But on this night, I was going to make Daddy talk to me. He needed to explain himself. I wasn't going to sneak out anymore if he was never going to talk to me again. Maybe, at the very least, he could talk to me like a psychic, which is when someone talks to you inside your brain and no one else can hear. Tater said he talked to his grandma like that sometimes, which was a little weird. But I met his grandma once and she didn't say anything, so I guess it made sense. Tater and I sat in his bedroom once to see if we could talk with our brains like that, but Tater said he couldn't hear my brain and we finally fell asleep.

The streetlights made it so I could look at myself in the window like a mirror. I could tell I was getting bigger. I made my arms into muscleman shapes. I imagined my fixed-up arm had superpowers and could break bad guys in half. I talked to my arm and said, "Let's do this."

I imagined a whole story happening in the window-mirror: A pig jumps at me, flying through the air, and my superpower arm points and turns it into a potato. And then I karate chop it and turn it into potato chips and eat it.

I tried to come up with a plan for getting in and out of the alley safely. Making plans is something you learn to do when you're a big kid. Making plans made me realize that my baby days were fading away. I felt proud, but I knew I was going to miss those days later—all those naps and boob milk.

My plan was to hide in the front part of the alley and listen really close for pig sounds. If I didn't hear anything, I'd go out and look around, and maybe see if I could find whatever Daddy wanted me to find. I'd count to ten and then hide again and listen some more, and then search again. I had just learned about ten. I thought this was a good and careful plan. Mom always said "Be careful."

There were a lot of places to hide in the alley, like behind garbage cans or shopping carts or mattresses. For some reason there were several mattresses leaning against things. There was a box of grown-up clothes and a suitcase with baby clothes in it. I took a bandana out, but it smelled like an old sock.

Next to one of the garbage cans was a wallet. There was no money inside, but there were several photos of a big brown dog. He was running in one of the pictures. Another one was of him on a beach somewhere. In one photo I could see someone's hand petting the dog's head. I was going to keep the pictures so I could pretend I had a real dog and not just the invisible one. I wanted to think that the hand in the photo was

Daddy's hand. This happened somewhere, I thought. Daddy and his dog. My dog now too. Maybe this was what Daddy wanted me to find.

Daddy was a thin sliver in the sky on this night. I held the photos up over my face and made silent psychic howls to Daddy—maybe to trick him, to wake him up, to make him look. I waited to hear if he would respond in my brain, but he didn't, so I barked out loud a couple of times. I was wearing black pants and a black shirt. Maybe he couldn't see me.

I folded the photos smaller and put them inside my pockets. I listened for pigs but didn't hear anything. I heard they smelled like bacon, but I didn't smell anything like that. Nothing good-smelling like bacon, anyway.

I felt safe, so I walked deeper into the alley. I'd never walked all the way through to the other side before, but I thought I could do it. To make myself not scared, I picked up a dirty carrot and made believe it was a gun. I'd forgotten to bring my bag, so I didn't have any snacks or toys with me. I didn't even have Ray for extra light. I heard music coming from the other end of the alley. It sounded like happy music, so I really wanted to get closer to it. Maybe there was a party there. It kind of sounded like Dad music.

I counted to ten and then hid and listened again. I was behind a big bag of garbage when I heard sounds coming from inside it. I didn't think they were pig sounds, but maybe it was a baby pig. I could probably defeat a baby pig, even if I didn't have a superpower arm. Everything got quiet again, so maybe it had fallen asleep. I didn't want to fight anything, even a baby pig. I held all of my breath inside me so that my nose breathing was silent, too, and I walked farther in, holding my carrot gun out in front of me. Ten seconds later I was hiding again, this time behind a stack of boxes. There was a sound coming from them, too, and it was even louder and squeakier. Maybe it was a bad decision to go into the alley after all. The pigs could be tricky, Dylan had told me. I looked back and saw something coming out of the garbage bag. Some kind of hairy hand. I thought it might be a werewolf or goblin. I stayed totally still and watched, but the hand sat there, unmoving. I tried to scoot behind the boxes more, but I bumped into one and made them all fall over. As the boxes were starting to tumble, I realized the hairy hand was a rat, and it jumped to the ground right before the boxes crashed loudly all around me. It must have been like a signal to every rat creature in the alley because a bunch of other ones leaped out of the boxes and scrambled around, bumping into each other as heads of lettuce, half-eaten sandwiches, and pieces of meat bounced off the ground by my feet. I ran straight for the other end of the alley. I didn't even look back or try to count how many there were or if they were chasing me or if they might actually be small pigs. I knew there were more than ten, though.

I finally got to the end of the alley, and I was on a street I didn't recognize. There were grown-ups lying down in blankets and sleeping bags down the whole sidewalk like it was a slumber party. One man had a radio on top of a newspaper box, and he was dancing in front of it like he was the only one who knew it was a party.

I looked up at Daddy, and he was there, glowing but silent, like nothing was happening, like he hadn't told me to go to the alley before.

"What?" I said to him.

No answer.

I didn't know where I was, but I decided to walk down the sidewalk in the direction of the moon so Daddy could see me and hopefully start talking to me. Maybe I would run into someone who could help me.

The man dancing to the radio saw me walking by and said, "Hey, Wilbur!"

I waved to him like I was Wilbur but kept walking. I saw a liquor store and a cigarette store and a tattoo store, and I still couldn't figure out where I was. A lot of stores looked empty. I looked in one window and saw a few broken chairs and some McDonald's bags scrunched up on the ground. One store had a cartoon pig's face on the window, but it didn't scare me because it was a cartoon and because it was smiling and wearing a hat like it was part human.

A woman with a dirty face was suddenly behind me and said, "This used to be a church. I used to sing here. I came back thinking I could sing here again and maybe they'd save me. Are you saved, baby?"

"No," I said, not really sure what "saved" meant. Maybe it was like on TV, when superheroes lifted people off the ground and flew away with them.

"I bet there's still a piano in there," she said.

"No Billy Joel," I said because it was the only thing I knew about pianos.

"Ah, Billy Joel," she said. "I don't hate it. But I like Billie Holiday or Billy Preston more. Come here and I'll show you something."

She took my hand and we walked to a doorway with a piece of wood nailed up where a door should have been. I liked how she treated me like a grown-up and wasn't calling the police or taking pictures of me with a phone. There were two backpacks under a blanket in the doorway, and she opened one and gave me a small blue radio. She dug around more and pulled out another one, a little bigger and silver.

"I collect these," she said. She turned mine on and a sad guitar sound came out. She turned hers on and it sounded like a bunch of trumpets and drums and bird sounds all mixed up. She placed the radios facing each other on the sidewalk and said, "Imagine what this sounds like with ten radios. This is how you speak to God, our father."

She took a deep breath and began singing words over the radio noise. Something about holy water and blood and shadows and lambs and fortresses. Some of the other people on the street made faces at her and told her to be quiet. I tried listening to her words in case she said something about Daddy, but she kept saying "Father" instead. She asked Father to forgive her and to bathe her in the river of mercy and then some stuff about snakes and demons and something about a poison apple, and it was kind of scary. When she looked up at the sky and her singing turned into angry yelling, I ran away.

People were saying bad words to her and there was a bunch of yelling and I hid behind a car with a flat tire. The radios got turned off and it was suddenly quiet again. I wondered if I was having a dream, it was so quiet. I pinched my arm and looked around to see where I should go. I heard her putting the radios back in her backpack and zipping it up. She called out, "You better get saved, baby. He died for your sins. Only He can give you everlasting life."

I looked under the car and saw her slippers getting closer, and then stop and stand there for a long time without moving. Then she said, "What was I doing now?" She walked back to her doorway and I snuck away.

I had to be careful as I walked farther down the street. Most of the streetlights didn't work, and there was broken glass and poop on the sidewalk too. And then there was no sidewalk, only dirt. I didn't know where I was, and I thought about turning around to find the alley again. I looked at Daddy and he was still just a sliver. I was hoping he might not hide as much if I went through the alley. I pulled out the photos and studied them more, thinking there might be clues to something. I held up the photo of the dog again and said, "Is this your dog?"

A car alarm went off somewhere close by, which made a dog start barking somewhere. Another dog barked and then another. It's what Mom would have called a racket. I kept walking on the dirt road. If I saw a light, I knew it would mean safety.

"Where now?" I said to Daddy. But there was silence, and I took more careful steps in the dark. It felt like a nightmare, being surrounded by so much darkness.

The only other times I had been in this much darkness was when Tater and I would play Womb Escape. That was a game Tater made up. We put all his blankets on top of us and we had to squirm around and pretend to be babies inside a mom, trying to get out. Tater said "fetuses," though, which is like a smaller baby shaped like a foot. We pretended we were crying fetuses when we played this game and it made our moms laugh so much that they'd end up really crying. It's funny how that could happen but sometimes be the other way around, where moms cried so much that they started laughing after they ran out of tears in their eyes. Tater said he remembered when he was a fetus and it was totally dark and nice. He said everyone should be used to darkness because that's all we see until we're shaped like regular babies and then come out of our moms' belly buttons.

It was so dark I couldn't even see my shoes. I could just keep going and make believe that I was playing a long game of Womb Escape. I knew the world was big, but I also knew it was round and there's a lot of water, so I would probably find something soon. I was getting hungry.

I walked for a while in the dark and then I started moaning because my stomach ached like I might poop, but I stopped and counted to ten and let out a fart. Someone laughed somewhere, and I said, "What's so funny?" to whoever was laughing.

"You're pretty brave," a voice said.

"Daddy?"

"Keep walking. You're almost there."

"There where?"

I saw the moon sliver get brighter. I hoped for an answer.

"Watch out," the voice said.

There was a box right in front of me that I was about to trip over. I opened it to see what was inside. It looked kind of like a computer. "What is it?" I asked, touching it carefully.

"A fax machine," the voice said. "Take it home and plug it in. Tell your mother to put paper in it."

"But, Daddy," I said. "Is this your fax machine?"

"Now walk home."

The fax machine was hard to carry, but the moonlight shined a path for me to follow, and the voice said, "Okay, now that way," and then "You're getting close to home."

I asked the voice if it was Daddy, and it said, "What do you think?"

I was getting so tired that I wanted to throw a tantrum like I'd seen other babies do sometimes. "Don't give up," the voice said. It sang "Danny Boy" but changed it to "Tony Boy."

Oh Tony boy, the pipes, the pipes are calling
From glen to glen, and down the mountain side
The summer's gone, and all the roses falling
'Tis you, 'tis you must go and I must bide

I walked until I got to a familiar building, and then I saw I was close to Banjo's. Dylan was standing out front with a carton of milk and a cigarette. I accidentally dropped the fax machine and it made a big crash sound. Dylan squinted over in my direction and ran over with the cigarette dangling from his mouth. He laughed and coughed at the same time.

"Dude, I thought you went to the moon or something," he said.

I looked up at the moon and saw it was hiding behind a thin cloud, its light dimming.

"What the hell you got there?" Dylan asked, pointing to the fax machine. He picked it up and shook it like a rattle. "A paper shredder?"

"Fax machine," I said. I wasn't really sure what it did, so I didn't say anything else.

"Oh, shit, little man. I don't think I've ever seen one before." He looked at it closer and blew smoke rings into the air. He glanced at the darkness behind me. "Were you hanging out on Washington Street? Kind of rough for a dude like you. I like your black clothes, though. Goth baby." He smiled and nodded and did a weird little dance.

I stood there, tired and sad. I wanted the voice to come back. I wanted to know if it was really Daddy. I wanted him to say my name like he knew me.

I looked at Dylan and wondered if he was anyone's dad. His hair was blue that night. He had a big Band-Aid on his neck. His T-shirt had a bad word on it.

"Up," I said.

Dylan picked me up and asked if I wanted to go home. I nodded but didn't feel like smiling. He walked in the direction that had more light.

"Fax machine," I said, and he turned around and went back to get it. He made a grunting sound like he was working really hard to pick it up.

"You owe me for this one," he said.

I felt myself starting to fall asleep and for some reason I said, "Chocolate cream pie."

Dylan laughed and said, "Yeah, that sounds like a fair trade. Next time your mom makes one of those, sneak it out to me."

18

MOM READ A BOOK called *Harold and the Purple Crayon* to me sometimes. It's about a baby who wants to walk in the moonlight but has to draw the moon in the sky so he can walk in its light. The book doesn't say that the moon is his dad, but the moon is on every page, watching Harold as he draws his own story. It never talks or hides behind clouds. It doesn't have a face.

Maybe there was a daddy hiding somewhere else in the book. When I imagined what Harold's mom looked like, she was always small and had a sad face. Maybe because Mom cried a little every time she read the story.

I didn't think it was a true story, though, because there were no garbage cans or alleys or Mexican food places. There were a lot of windows, though. Harold draws so many of them in the book, even though he knows they're not his window. I imagined what could be on the other side of the windows. Maybe other babies he could be friends with. Maybe pianos or TVs. There is a dragon in the book, but only at the beginning. The book says the dragon is scary, but it wasn't really scary to me. Maybe there were scarier ones in all the windows Harold draws, in all those tall buildings that he almost gets lost in at the end.

It made me remember one time when me and Mom were waiting for a bus somewhere and there were tall buildings all around us, and it seemed like we were waiting for a long time and she kept saying things like, "I thought it would be here by now," and "Maybe we missed it." And she was holding me against her shoulder and bouncing a little so when I made a burp or a sound, it would bounce, too, and sound funny in her ear and make her giggle. I kept looking up at a big window, and there was a person up there looking down at me and waving. I didn't know who it was, but in my mind their name was Droopy. Their face looked like a mask and kind of like it was melted in parts. Their eyes looked crooked and their nose was hard to see, and their lips were big and sort of falling off into their neck. They moved back and forth behind a curtain like peekaboo. Another person came to the window and waved too, and they had on big sunglasses and long black hair that looked like a wig. The way this person was waving looked like they were waving at someone else farther away. It was hard to tell where they were waving, but then they stopped and stood there like a statue, while Droopy kept waving and playing peekaboo. In another window was a giant dog, watching me with his tongue out. He was standing up on his hind legs like a human. I thought maybe he was a naked man. And then in another window, an old lady laughed while sticking her finger in her nose. I put my finger in my nose, too, because it made me laugh. She stopped laughing and fell backwards. When I looked at the other windows again, they were empty.

Listening to Mom read *Harold and the Purple Crayon* always made me remember those people in the windows, but also made me wonder if they were real or imaginary, like the windows Harold makes. I think Harold is making all those purple windows for a reason, but then he's too scared to look in them. When he makes his window at the end, he makes sure he puts the moon right in the middle so he can see it from his bed, like it will protect him. It's his favorite window. It's a happy ending.

THREE YEARS OLD

19

ME AND TATER were at the park, burying superheroes in the sand. One of them was named Awkward Man. He had a gold shirt and a pitchfork and was supposed to live in the water where he could breathe better. Tater said he was dying because he was buried in lava with only his arm and pitchfork sticking out. Another superhero was Sharkman. I think he used to be a bad guy, but we made him a good guy because he looked cool and decided to switch sides. He was buried up to his fin. Tater said Sharkman eats lava for breakfast and then pooped it on his enemies to kill them.

"No more killing," Tater's mom said. She was watching us because Mom was doing something with Ben out in the country. That's what she said, anyhow. I wasn't sure what made the country so special, but maybe it was because they rode horses out there. I hoped they were wearing cowboy hats. I'd always wanted my own cowboy hat because they made me laugh for some reason.

"He's not really going to die!" Tater yelled over to his mom. He pulled Awkward Man out of the sand and pretended he was coughing up sand. "Water. Water. Water," he said, but like in a superhero voice. Tater dropped him back in the sand.

"Don't tell my mom he's dead," he said to me. He seemed kind of sad about it, but he had a smile on his face.

"Don't tell my mom," I said back.

"Don't tell her what?" Tater said.

"Daddy's in the alley," I said.

"Ew," Tater said. "That's gross. I'm glad my dad's not in the alley."

"I got a fax machine," I said. I was hoping Tater might be able to show me how to use it.

"That's cool," he said. "My dad has a fax machine. He gets fax all the time. He's good at it."

"I wanna be good at it," I said.

"You push buttons and it sends messages into a cloud," he said.

"Wow," I said. "Awesome."

I'd recently started using the word *awesome* and it made me feel like I was as smart as Tater. *Awesome* means something that is the best and most powerful—way better than *good*.

Tater's mom was doing something on her phone. She kept putting the phone in her pocket and then pulling it out and pushing buttons. Mom once told me that some people like writing more than talking, so they spell out messages on their phones. That way they could think about their words more and didn't have to open their mouths. I guess that makes a phone kind of like a fax machine but smaller.

Tater would shout to his mom sometimes for no reason, and she'd smile and do binocular hands and say, "I got you in my scope, kiddos!" There were about ten other kids at the park, but we were the smallest ones. The bigger kids were climbing up high on things and pretending they had guns. All the parents stood around and made sour-looking faces when any of the kids made a shooting sound. But it didn't sound real, so they let them do it while looking around all nervous. One time an older kid had something called a cap gun and it made firecracker sounds and even a stinky smoke smell. The police came and took it away from him and said it looked too real. Then everyone wanted to see the *real* real police guns they carried, but instead they gave everyone baseball cards for a team no one had ever heard of.

"Who's hungry for kumquats?" said somebody walking up. It was that Chad man again. A couple of the parents called their kids over and packed up their stuff like they were in a hurry. Tater's mom frowned and walked over to where we were.

"Oh, hello," Chad said to her. He nodded at us and said, "I know these young gentlemen."

"So do I," she said. "I'm this one's mother." She squeezed Tater's shoulder.

"He gave us jackalope once," said Tater.

Chad laughed. "That was jackfruit. Jackalopes aren't real. They're only in comic books and dreams." He shook a paper bag in his hands. "I got a new treat today, though, if you think you can handle it."

He opened the bag and showed us. There was a plastic bag with tiny oranges inside it.

"Can we have one, Mom?" Tater asked.

"What are they again?" she asked.

"These are kumquats," Chad said. "They look like miniature oranges, but you can eat the skin on 'em too. I like to pop them in my mouth and eat them whole like a grape. They're kind of tart, though."

He gave one to Tater's mom, and she smelled it and then put it in her mouth. She made a funny face and then swallowed.

"Well, I'm still alive," she said.

Chad smiled and offered us a smaller one, cut in half. I put my tongue on it. It tasted like sour orange juice. Tater chewed on his piece but then spit it into his hand.

"It tastes bad," he said. He ran to the water fountain.

Chad's face looked sad, like he'd just lost a game. I put my piece in my pocket and pretended like I was eating it. "I like it," I said.

Chad looked at me and smiled. I'd always wanted to be one of those grown-ups who could eat any weird food.

"You have very good taste," he said. "Have another one!"

He opened the plastic bag, and I grabbed another half of one. I'd only lied to make him feel better, but I guess lies sometimes made bad things happen, because then I had to eat another piece of food that tasted like an extra-sour piece of rubber. I put it in my mouth and tried to ignore what it was doing in there. He watched me and smiled and ate another one himself.

"I'm Chad, by the way," he said to Tater's mom. "I used to be a farmer. I only eat healthy, organic foods. I've been exploring the world of fruits lately. I think it's important to always explore, even when you're older like me. Don't you agree?"

Tater's mom looked like she was trying to figure out what the question was and if she was going to agree with it.

"Oh, sure, sure," she said. "I'm always exploring. Looking for the big answers to life."

I couldn't keep it in my mouth any longer. I spat the weird food into my hand and crammed it in my pocket. It felt like two dead slugs in there. Tater made me hold slugs once, so I knew what they felt like.

"And the big questions are important too," Chad said. "I'm almost jealous of those kids, that they have so much time left to think and explore."

"You have a lot of time left, too, I bet," she said. "My dad once said that retirement was like a second childhood."

"I did retire this year," he said.

"Well, there you go," she said. "Eating exotic fruit and walking through a park. You got a good start on it."

Neither of them said anything for a while. I sat close by, playing with Sharkman and a toy spaceship. Tater was on the jungle gym, dropping his shoes off the highest part and watching them bounce off the ground.

Chad cleared his throat and reached up to stretch his arms over his head. He grabbed his ears and tugged on them. "I'm invisible," he said.

Tater's mom looked at him and tilted her head like she was confused. "What?"

I looked, too, but he wasn't invisible at all. I could see him, easy.

"Here's how it goes," he said. "Part one: I'm old. Part two: I don't have a job anymore. Part three: I have inoperable brain cancer. Part four: I'm dying."

Tater's mom looked like she was holding her breath. Her hands moved to her face like she was going to cover her eyes. "Oh, I'm so sorry." She said it slowly, like she had to think a lot about each word when she said it, like she wasn't sure they were the right words.

"My daddy always said life is short," Chad said.

I wondered about his daddy. Did he live with him or is he something in the sky, too—a smaller moon or a star? If someone didn't have a daddy they lived with, could they still see them somewhere? I knew some people went to the place with graves and big pieces of rock sticking out of the grass, and they talked to the ground there. Or sometimes they went out on boats and talked to the water. Nobody had taught me all the things that could be a daddy, but I was starting to think they were everywhere: all the dogs and cats, some trees, those big signs with smiling old people on them, the naked-guy statue in churches, ceiling fans, rainbows, the wind. One time I saw a man in a big, long car and he made the engine growl really loud and said to the steering wheel, "Yeah, talk to me, Daddy."

"Do you have someone to take care of you?" Tater's mom asked. "I mean, someone to help?"

"I have some help," Chad said. "I have a partner, but no one else knows, not even my daughters."

I heard a bird singing somewhere. Tater's mom looked like she was crying and trying to hide her face.

I feel worried when grown-ups cry. Sometimes they get so quiet. When I'm sad, I get louder. I want everyone to hear me cry. I only get quiet when I'm scared. Maybe Tater's mom was sad and scared at the same time.

Chad held a napkin out to her. She took it and blew her nose with it.

"I shouldn't have told you," he said. "Sometimes it's easier to tell strangers your secrets, I guess."

I didn't understand everything they were talking about, but I knew it must have been serious. Tater was shouting at me to save him. He was stuck in the middle of the slide.

"Hurry up, before I die!" he yelled.

I ran over and climbed up to the top of the twisty slide. I sat down and pushed off, sliding down the yellow plastic and crashing into Tater.

"Okay, are you ready?" he said. "We're inside the monster's stomach. We have to get pooped out and then we can kill it with our spike hands."

We wiggled down the slide slowly, squeaking and grunting. Tater made a fart sound with a real fart when we got to the bottom. We were laughing so hard it sounded like crying. Tater's mom looked over at us but saw we were just cracking up. Tater's stomach made a waterfall kind of sound.

"That Chad food is weird," he said. "Watch. I bet he tries to kiss my mom."

I looked at them, but they were only talking and nodding.

Then Tater's mom gave Chad a hug and patted him on the back like she was burping him.

"Told ya," Tater said. "He's a dirty old man."

"Dirty man?" I said.

"Yeah, a real doggy dog."

Tater's mom picked up our stuff and shouted, "Let's go, guys! We got a schedule to keep."

We walked over to them, and I kept waiting for Chad to kiss Tater's mom like Tater said he would. I thought about kissing Tater's mom once. She kissed me on the head when I had my first birthday, but I didn't kiss her back.

"Before we go," Tater's mom said, "Please say thank you to Mr. Chad."

Grown-ups always tell kids to say thank you. I didn't really know what it meant for a long time, but you always have to stop what you're doing to say it. I would try to say it as fast as I could so people didn't have to wait around. There was a bird at the pet store that could say it and it was like he was showing off.

We said thank you to Chad. He smiled and bowed. I noticed that his teeth were kind of gray but his eyes were bright blue and nice, like he used to be a president or something important like that.

"Can you tell me something?" he asked. I didn't know what to tell him, and Tater looked around like he was forgetting something.

Chad whispered low and serious, like he didn't even want the birds to hear, "What is the most important thing in your life?"

"Oh, I know!" Tater said. "The computer I play my games on. Plus, my mom and dad. Plus, the sun."

"Well, okay, then," Chad said. Then he turned to me. "What about you? What is the most important thing in your life?"

I thought about all the things that were important: Mom, Tater, my apple bell, Ray, my Velcro shoes, my bed, my Lego toys, my stuffies, my Hot Wheels, Daddy. If "important" means you think about it a lot, I guess Daddy would have been in the lead. Daddy. The moon.

But I was afraid to say that for some reason. Instead I said, "Nothing."

20

I LEARNED HOW to say more words with my mouth. It felt like a lot, and it was getting easier and easier, like my brain was finally teaching my mouth how to say things like a big kid.

Mom was making breakfast one morning when I said, "Have you ever witnessed a real alligator?"

I don't know how the word *witnessed* came into my head, or even *alligator*. I'd never even practiced saying such a long word. I even impressed myself.

Mom almost choked on her orange juice and then gave me a long look like she was trying to figure out who I was. Then she said calmly, "In fact, Tony, I have. One time I even came close to being attacked by one. You have to be careful, especially around waterways. The one I saw was in a drained-out ditch. I ran out of there as fast as I could."

"How fast did you run?" I asked.

"Faster than the alligator," she said.

"Of course," I said. I liked saying "of course" any chance I got. It made me feel smart, like a schoolkid. It even made me feel taller somehow when I said it, like I could see over things.

Mom didn't even write down my new words in her notebook anymore. It was up on a bookshelf, next to a big book about wizards she said I could read when I was older. There was also a big book of outer space pictures—not only the moon and the clouds and the places where airplanes fly, but also planets, asteroids, stars, UFOs, rockets, and big glowing swirly parts you aren't supposed to get close to. Sometimes I looked through this book and dreamed about all the adventures out there, and if Daddy was going to tell me about them someday. On the nights when the moon disappeared, I thought Daddy must be at these other places.

There was one page in the book that showed a bunch of different pictures of the moon, starting when it's a big, full, glowing circle and then slowly fading, like someone was erasing more and more of it until it was fingernail-shaped. I'd seen all those different Daddy faces in the sky, but it was nice to also see them in this book if I wanted to think about him. The pictures were more close-up, and when I looked at the ones where he was disappearing, I could almost see a little more of him, like he was just hiding behind a black curtain.

There were two pictures in the book that kind of scared me. One where he looked orange or red, like maybe he'd heated up to a hot temperature. Mom said that was called a Bloody Moon, and it made me wonder if Daddy got bloody sometimes, like from a fight or getting poked with a knife or an asteroid. The other scary moon picture looked like a big white zero in the dark, like it was surrounded by white fire. I asked Mom why, and she said it's when the moon goes in front of the sun and blocks most of the light but the sun is much bigger so you can still see its bright outline. She also said I should never look at the sun, even with my sunglasses on. I had heard some people say the sun was good for you, but other people said it was bad for you. Mom said it's four hundred times bigger than the moon but it's farther away, so no one has flown a rocket there yet. One time a man flew to the moon and walked on it. A dog and a monkey also flew there, but they crashed and maybe died. Nobody ever found out. Tater told me there were worms and turtles and robots that had gotten close to living there. I bet worms were already there, and maybe bees.

If I ever go there, I bet I could find the dog and the monkey. They'd probably be excited to have someone to play catch-the-ball with.

One time Ben was looking at the space book and flipping the pages really fast like he was angry or something. "Why do you even have this?" he shouted toward Mom, who was in the kitchen.

"It's educational," she said. "Plus, Tony likes it."

I always liked it when she said my name to someone when I was close by. Sometimes if I saw someone say a dog's name when the dog was close by, it looked up and wagged its tail and got happy. I understood that. I would smile and wag my tail if I had one.

Ben sniffed the book and said, "It smells bad."

Mom stuck her head in the room and said, "You smell bad."

Ben didn't like that, I could tell. "There's only one of us here that smells," he said, looking at me.

"Yeah, and it's you," Mom said to him.

I laughed, and Mom gave me a high five, and then Ben laughed, even though he was kind of the joke. He kept looking at the book with a funny face, like he was sick from something that changed his face so it wouldn't look normal anymore. He shook his head and then stared at me like he was trying to make my face sick too. But I kept my face as normal as possible.

"Hey, Tony," he said. "How'd you like to live on Uranus? It says here it has over twenty moons. Think about that."

He closed the book and tiptoed out of the room with it. When he came back, he didn't have the book. He wiped his hands on his pants, like the pages had gotten bad germs on him.

I did think about all those moons, though. It was exciting to imagine a sky with so many moons, like a bunch of flashlights shining down on me. Could I tell them apart? Would Daddy still be one of them? Or *on* one? Would he talk to me or be too shy with all the other moons around? Would the moons fight each other? I imagined living on Uranus but taking vacations on the moons, like they were islands. Were there islands in space? Or do you basically go from one moon or planet to the next? I thought about what it would be like to eat space food and how it would float in the air for anyone to grab. I wondered if there would be Uranus people who would get mad about us eating their food. I bet people wear glow-in-the-dark socks on Uranus.

Mom found the space book under the towels in the bathroom closet a week later. She put it back on the bookshelf, right by my notebook of words.

I felt proud that I knew so many words that they probably couldn't fit in the notebook. But I liked looking up there and knowing that if I forgot some of my first words, I could always figure out how to climb up and get it. And that I could also get the space book whenever I wanted. I knew the pictures held valuable secrets, like a map to a hidden treasure.

21

I'M NOT SURE if Mom knew what the fax machine was supposed to be for or where it came from, but because she could see that I was really interested in it, she put it in my room and plugged it in.

"If I can figure out what the fax number is, maybe I'll even send you a fax from work," she said. "I may have to watch a YouTube video to figure out how to send a fax."

Sometimes we watched YouTube videos to learn things, like when we had to stop our smoke alarm from chirping or when Mom made a teething ring.

I liked pushing buttons on the fax machine and then picking up the phone like I was talking to someone. I drew pictures on pieces of paper and put them in the tray and made electricity sounds like I was sending a message. Most of the pictures were moons or rats or superheroes.

I tried to figure out if I could play any computer games on it, but it didn't work that way. There was no screen, and only a few sounds came out.

Days went by, and I was worried that I'd never know how to use it. Mom seemed to forget about it and never actually tried to send me a fax. I got bored of looking at it, waiting for it to do something fun.

But late one night a green light blinked on the machine,

and it made a squealing sound from somewhere inside. It sounded like a small bird being squished in and out like a squeeze toy, and it scared me awake. A piece of paper with some kind of writing came out of the machine, but the letters were big and sloppy, like a kid had written it. I couldn't read it, but the letters were H-E-L-P. And there was a smiley face on it too.

I put on my coat and shoes and made sure Mom wasn't awake. I folded up the fax message and put it in my coat pocket. I unlocked the apartment door and ran down the hall and out the front door.

I saw a man smoking on the corner by a pay phone. This was the only pay phone I'd seen in the city. Mom tried to explain to me how it worked once, but I didn't understand. You put money in a phone? Why was there a little glass office for this phone? How come some of the glass was broken into tiny pieces? Why was there a devil face painted on the phone?

There were a lot of unanswered questions. Still, it must be an important phone, even though I'd never heard it ring. Maybe it was like a fax machine but with fewer buttons.

I walked up to the man and startled him so much that he stumbled back and fell off the sidewalk. I felt bad about this because he was wearing a nice suit and now it was dirty.

"Where the fuck did you come from?" he said. He looked like a serious businessman and his hair was gray like a daddy's daddy. "I don't care who or what you are!" he shouted. "You don't walk up all quiet to someone at this time of night! Now, what do you want?"

I held out the fax message for him. I was hoping he could tell me what it said. "Can you read this?" I asked.

"I never give handouts," he said with a mean face. "You have to work for your money, kid. Even someone your age can shine shoes or sell drugs or whatever."

"I'm only three years old," I told him.

"Well, you look and sound old for your age," he said. "Now get away from here before you get into more trouble."

I walked down the street some more, looking up to see if Daddy was around and could help me. But he wasn't out, at least not in the sky. There was a broken fire hydrant on the next corner and a couple of women were letting it spray on them like they were taking a shower. They rubbed the water on their faces and then washed each other's backs. It looked like they were only wearing their underwear.

Someone stopped me before I got too close. "Hey, aren't you La-La's baby?"

It was a woman with gold teeth and tattoos on her face. I'd seen her before. Sometimes during the day she asked for one-dollar bills in front of the food store. She held a little dog in a blanket in her arms, but it didn't look alive. It looked like one of those dogs that used to be alive but was filled with teddy bear stuffing after it died. I stared at the dog's eyes once, but they looked like marbles and they didn't move.

"No," I said to the woman. "I'm looking for Daddy."

"Oh, you belong to Dylan, right?" She looked worried but also annoyed.

"Where is the moon?" I asked.

"Who told you about moon?" she said. "You don't want no moon. Did Dylan send you out?"

She looked at the note in my hand and laughed a little. Not like a joke laugh, but like a sound you make when you want something to be funny but it's not even close.

"You better hold on to that," she said. "You might need it."

"Daddy," I said.

"Your daddy ain't shit, making you look for moon. Come with me. We're going to fix this."

The woman picked me up and I let her, even though I was

confused. I don't know why she had to tell me that Daddy wasn't poop. But what if he is? Maybe Daddy *was* a piece of poop. Maybe in the alley. I'd heard stories about people changing into things like statues or angels or dust. But poop was pretty bad.

The woman carried me to an old building with a sharp wire fence around it. We slipped through an open part where the fence had been twisted away from a post and walked quickly into one of the open doorways. There were no lights on but there were a couple of small fires making some light. The insides looked like our apartment building but without all the walls put up. I once heard Mom say that it was supposed to be a new place for people to live in, but the workers ran out of money and didn't finish. I think this happened before I was born. I think almost everything in our city happened before I was born.

We walked over to a sleeping bag with someone in it, and she set me down. A hubcap was on the ground by the zipped-up sleeping bag, and the woman leaned down and picked up a small shiny thing that looked like a rock.

"Don't ever touch this nasty shit," she whispered to me. "This is the worst thing that's ever shown up on this street." She put it in her pocket and then kicked the sleeping bag. Nothing happened.

"Shit," I said quietly.

Then the sleeping bag wiggled like a worm, and I heard the zipper zip open. Someone with pink hair like cotton candy stuck their head out. It was Dylan.

"What is your problem?" he said to the woman.

"I don't know if you're making this kid do your dirty deeds," she said, "but he was out there with a damn sign that said HELP, and when I asked him what he needed help with, he said he was looking for moon. I can only guess who put him up to that!"

Dylan belched and opened his eyes enough to finally notice me. "He's looking for *the* moon," he said. He lifted his arms out of the bag and squirmed out. "His name's Tony, and I don't make him do anything. He's straight edge, anyway."

"Is he yours?" she asked him.

"No," Dylan said. "I mean, yeah. I mean, I don't know. Let me wake up. Jesus." He looked at me like he was angry, like I had done something wrong.

"Well, get him out of here," she said. "And tell him to stop asking about moon."

22

DYLAN TOOK ME to a doughnut shop down the street. He counted out some coins in his hands as I looked at all the doughnuts with their pretty frosting: red, blue, yellow, pink, white, and orange. They sparkled under the lights. It was so bright in there, it reminded me of the time I was born. I remember that day because it was the first time I came out of the dark place where I had grown up inside Mom and into a room full of people wearing all-white clothes under lights as blinding as giant flashlights in my face. It was the most pain I ever had in my eyes.

"You got any money?" Dylan asked me.

I reached in my jacket pocket and found a nickel. Dylan grabbed it and said, "Let's look at the day-olds." The frosting on the day-olds was not as pretty and a fly was buzzing over them. Dylan bought three of the them, and we sat at one of the little tables. He gave me a booster seat and a doughnut with red, white, and blue sprinkles. On his napkin was a maple bar and glazed doughnut that looked like a plain bagel. I bit into my doughnut and most of the sprinkles fell onto my shirt and pants.

"What are you doing with your life?" Dylan said.

I wasn't sure what he meant or why he wanted to know. "Eating a doughnut," I said.

Dylan lifted his hands to his head and squeezed. His hands looked really giant and his head seemed like a little ball. He could have squeezed his whole face if he wanted to.

"No. No. I'm talking to myself," he said.

There was no one else in the doughnut shop except for the man working behind the counter, who was drinking coffee and reading a book with an outer space alien on the cover.

"Tony, listen to me," Dylan said. "You like stories, right? I need to tell you a few things so you can do better than me. I mean, you're young and you'll have experiences, but I don't want you to go down the path I took. I think you can avoid it if you're smart, and I think you're probably smart."

His skin looked sweaty and green, and his hands were shaking. An old woman came in the shop talking loudly, asking for two whole boxes to go. She stood there wobbling like she was dizzy, but she smiled like she was having fun. She dropped her purse when she was trying to pay and then, on her way out, looked at us and said to Dylan, "I like to see a good dad taking care of his child. It's not every day."

Dylan tried to make himself smile like a dad and waved to the lady as she slipped back into the dark.

"I didn't even have a dad," he said to me. "I mean, I had a stepdad once for six months, but that wasn't good at all. I probably could have used a real one, but my mom said he died the week I was born. She told me it was heat stroke. But I found out later that he was addicted to meth. So I don't think he died of heat stroke, unless he passed out somewhere in the sun.

"I always felt alone when I was a kid. I didn't even have babysitters. I don't think my mom could afford it. When I was about twelve, she got married to some guy, but I never even knew his name. He wanted me to call him Captain. I think he was a cop, but I'm not sure. Maybe a security guard. He wore a uniform like that, with a badge and walkie-talkie. One day my mom put it on like she was playing a joke, and he freaked out and beat her up. After that we lived in our car for about a year. I missed almost all of sixth grade. Then my mom won some money somehow. She said it was from a bet. I'm not sure what she bet on. Maybe the Olympics. She was really into swimming. We'd sneak into the public pool at night and she'd teach me to swim, and I was really good, actually. Faster than her, even.

"Anyway, she won some money and we moved into my uncle's garage. It doesn't sound like much, but things were looking up. I finally got clothes that fit and went back to school. I tried out for a swim team at the Boys & Girls Club, and they let me join for free because I was the best in my age group. But I didn't like rules and schedules for some reason. I mean, it's not that hard, but I was lazy.

"I stopped going to practice. I went to the bowling alley and played video games with quarters I'd kind of steal from other kids. And then these three older kids gave me free quarters if I delivered stuff to this music store down the street—brown bags of cassette-tape boxes, like these little plastic squares. But there were no cassettes in them. I was so dumb I thought these things wrapped up inside had something to do with music.

"One day, some guys on motorcycles rode up to me and swiped one of the bags out of my hand. I told the kids at the bowling alley, and they didn't believe me. They said if my story was true I'd be beaten up or something. They got mad and pushed me against a wall, and one of them tried to choke me. I yelled but no one could hear me because of all the noise of the bowling balls and pins and shit. They said I'd have to do extra work, and if I did it, we'd be square.

"I didn't want to go back there after that. So I went back to swim practice, but they had already kicked me off the team. I had to find a new place to go, and I thought the mall would be a safe place. I figured I could find somewhere to hide in there if I ever saw any of the bowling alley kids. I didn't see them for a long time, but one day they saw me in a 7-Eleven. They covered their faces and attacked me—tipped over a big display of chips and salsa on me. Held me down and threw hot dogs and Slurpees on me. They ran out, and the old lady working there called the cops and told me to stay. She was freaking out and having a hard time breathing. When the cops showed up, she told them I started the fight, so they arrested me and told me I'd have to pay for the damages to the store. They handcuffed me and had to wipe all the crap off me with towels before they put me in their car. One of them spit on a napkin and wiped my face with it and laughed. Fucking pig."

I noticed the man behind the counter looking at us with an angry face. "Don't talk shit, man. Pigs keep me in business," he said.

Dylan looked at the man and shook his head. The man laughed and looked at his phone and then went back to reading.

"My mom," Dylan said, taking a bite of his doughnut, "she was cool about it at first, but then she finds out everything— that I was skipping practice, that I was making these drug deliveries, that I was kicked off the team. But the thing that messed me up the most was that she believed that I stole that bag of drugs. Like, she didn't know that *I didn't know* what I was doing. It got all twisted. I guess these were choices I made, but, you know, it felt more like these things happened *to* me. I had bad luck. It started off small but got a lot bigger. So I had to go to juvie for two months, which wasn't so bad now that I think about it, even though some kid hit me with a tray on the second day and chipped my front tooth."

He lifted his lip and showed me the tooth. It was tiny and weird-looking.

"When I got out, my mom was starting to do drugs, too, and she was actually working for those bowling alley kids. But also, I figured out that those kids weren't really kids. They were, like, thirty years old. They just dressed and acted like teenagers.

"Things were bad, man. It was so freakin' bad. So I ran away for the first time. I stole some new clothes and changed my hair and walked for, I don't know, like a week, to some town I'd never heard of before. It was called Shelton, and some grandpa guy with a big beard picked me up and said he'd give me a job and give me food and stuff. His name was Peck and he had a big farm, with chickens and goats and cattle. He even had a chimp, but I don't think he had a license for it or whatever. The chimp had a French name. I could never say it right, and I was scared of it anyway.

"It was such a weird time being out there, man. I mean, *good* weird. Really special. It almost seems like a dream now. That old man took care of me like a son, but even closer than a son. He said he had a daughter, but she lived in a hospital for some reason and never came around. He said the rest of his family had fancy jobs and lots of money but were still unhappy. He said life should be simple, and he was right. He made me think of the word *wise*. He seemed full of wisdom and shit. But also like a mountain man, like he didn't belong in the current world. He listened to classical music and tried to teach me how to play violin. He fed me healthy food and taught me a lot—kind of homeschooled me for a couple of years. There were these old newspapers around, and he'd make me read those and then test me on them. I didn't always understand them, but it was cool.

"There weren't any neighbors or other kids around. It was lot of open fields and some woods we'd hike through sometimes. But a lady cop came out to the farm one day and asked him if he was keeping a chimp, and Peck had to pretend he didn't know anything about it. Told the cop he saw Bigfoot once and some giant possums, but no chimp had ever been on his land. I had to hide in the canning room while she was there because I didn't have any kind of ID and I wasn't sure if I was wanted for a crime or whatever. Maybe my mom wrote me off or maybe there were Wanted signs up with my face on them.

"I heard them talking, and the cop asked Peck if he had kids or someone living with him, and Peck told her no and started to lose his patience. He said he never caused any trouble and paid his taxes and worked his land so he could live a peaceful life. It was a good speech, what parts of it I could hear. The chimp was sleeping in a tree right by the house while this all happened. The police lady told Peck there was a complaint from someone in the community and that she might have to come back with a search warrant and some animal control people to look around soon.

"When she drove off, the chimp jumped down from the tree and Peck just broke down in tears. He knew he could get into a lot of trouble with me and a chimp living there. I told him I could take the chimp and hide in the woods when they came back. He was really sad the rest of the day, but the next morning we made a plan. He packed a suitcase for us, and we walked into the woods, looking for the best hiding spots. I could tell the chimp was confused about what was happening, and Peck would say these French words to him as we walked off trail with machetes through these wild branches and bushes.

"We found a huge tree that had a hollowed-out part on the bottom, and Peck had the chimp sit inside it to see if it was big enough to hide in. It was . . . barely. We rested there for a few minutes, and before we hid the suitcase, the chimp opened it to see what was inside. It had some clothes for both of us, a gallon of water, some dried fruits, a pack of cards, a radio, a homemade map, and some matches. The chimp closed the suitcase and looked right at Peck and made this kind of grunting sound. Peck started talking French to him, but the chimp picked up the suitcase and smashed him right in the face with it. I was yelling for him to stop and tried to grab the suitcase away, but the chimp threw me off like I was nothing. My machete was lost in the brush. All I could do was watch the chimp tear away at Peck. Clothes and blood going everywhere. People say chimps can tear your arms off, and this one was barely bigger than you, but it was, um . . . I don't know. It was a beast. It was a demon. It was crazy, and I couldn't do anything but run away. I heard Peck shouting, saying the chimp's name over and over until he finally stopped. I wish I knew how to say the chimp's name.

"I ran through the woods for a long time, and it was totally quiet, but I didn't want to slow down until I was back at the house safe. I knew I should disappear, but I didn't want to leave. I thought if I stayed there, Peck would come back and be okay, maybe with some scratches and bandages. But I knew deep down that he was probably dead. I didn't know if the chimp was coming back to the house, so I found Peck's gun and loaded it just to be safe. That chimp could open doors, climb through windows . . . anything. I found some money Peck had stashed away and packed the biggest backpack with clothes and got out of there.

"I walked for a couple of days, and then some dude picked me up in his car and drove me straight to a homeless shelter. I made up a story and told him I couldn't be around people yet, so he took me to a park instead. I don't know if he was a priest or anything, but he asked me to confess to whatever I had done. By this time, I thought everything was my fault, but I really didn't know. He said he knew I did something bad, and I just broke down. He put his hand on my leg like he was trying to comfort me, and then it felt like he was searching for something. He moved his hand up until he could feel the money in my pocket. He said if I gave him all the money, he would pretend like he'd never met me. You know what he said to me?"

I was confused by Dylan's question. How would I know what he said? This is something that happened all the time: people asking me if I know something that I don't know but they already know what it is! I'm not sure why people ask questions like that. I almost said, "I don't know," but I didn't think Dylan actually wanted me to say anything, so I waited.

"He said, 'You deserve this. I never met a good kid hitchhiking before. Only bad kids.' That's what he said to me, and I thought he was probably right, so I handed over my money. Maybe like nine hundred bucks. He let me keep five dollars. I slept in the park that night but kept waking up because I thought the chimp was spying on me somehow. When I finally did fall asleep, my backpack was stolen. I had one of my arms through the straps while I slept, but they cut through the fabric. I saw the straps on the grass next to me but no sign of the rest of my stuff. I was back to having nothing, nowhere to go and no friends. It was worse than the time when I was twelve and sleeping in a car with my mom. Now I was fifteen and alone—too old for people to want to help, but too young to get a job. I stayed away from shelters and all the places where homeless people are. I knew I should, like, talk or whatever with other people, but I was afraid to meet anyone because I didn't know if the cops were looking for me. Dylan's not even my real name."

"What's your real name?" I asked.

"I'll tell you someday," he said.

The guy behind the counter got up and pushed some buttons on the coffee maker. "You want the rest of this coffee, bro? I gotta make a new pot."

"Thanks, man. That would be sweet," Dylan said.

The guy brought over a paper cup. I saw the smoke of the coffee rise in front of Dylan's face. It reminded me of Daddy in the clouds. It smelled like burnt wood.

"You guys have to leave in fifteen minutes," the guy said. "Can't stay here all night, especially when the morning rush starts."

Dylan gave the guy a salute and took a sip from the cup. The guy pointed at the clock and walked away.

I wished the coffee smoke would float to me, right into my face, so I could feel what it was like to be in a cloud. I had no idea why so many people liked drinking coffee, though. I didn't get the purpose of a drink being hot. It didn't seem safe to me.

Dylan continued his story.

"I kept out of sight for a long time. I slept in people's toolsheds, behind grocery stores on the loading docks, in cars, under cars. I even found an empty swimming pool in an old man's backyard to crash in. But I got lonely, man. As much as people made me nervous, I knew I had to make one friend at least. People talk about a support system, but I didn't even have one lousy person for a while.

"Then I met this skateboarder kid named Five-five because he was five foot five, and we became tight. He had some way to get money and food, but I wasn't sure how. He liked that I showed him these secret spots to sleep. He didn't like the crowded streets and he didn't trust people either. One time we stole a boat and floated on it to the next state. We caught some fish and then tried to figure out how to cook them. It was pretty gross, dude.

"Anyway, there was this really muscular bald guy who would randomly show up and drive Five-five somewhere, and this guy was giving him some kind of pills and Five-five got really into them. He got a cell phone and would text this guy sometimes and it really bugged me. I yelled at him for trusting this dude, but Five-five said he'd actually known him longer than he'd known me. He said I could maybe hang out with him, too, and then I'd have *two* friends.

"So one day we all hung out at this guy's house and it was pretty cool. We watched some funny videos, listened to music, played with his cats, shit like that. They took these yellow pills, but I said no. He let me drink beer instead, but it made me tired and feel sick. They were smiling so much and sort of making fun of me, so I decided I would take some pills too. I was, like, trying to fit in or whatever. You understand that, Tony? Fitting in is not usually a good thing in these situations. But I did it and I liked it. I liked it too much.

"The bald guy said his name was Mr. Clean, and he did become my second friend. Maybe not the right kind of friend, but I didn't know it yet. Mr. Clean had other friends, and they acted like they were our friends too. Five-five and I slept at his house sometimes, and we'd have what we called friend parties. Sometimes the other friends would give us money and other drugs. It was almost like they were paying us to take drugs with them. I was becoming an addict, but I didn't even know it. My body was changing. That's how you know when you have a problem. Your body feels like a slimy leather suit over your skeleton."

I thought about my skeleton and how my skin was maybe a

suit. I rubbed my arm where there used to be a cast. I looked at Dylan's face and could almost see his skull.

"Then one night I stole some of the pills. And they came looking for me. Five-five said I was in trouble and he couldn't be my friend anymore. I was scared, but I was high too. I finally came out here and met some other dealers and street folks. They could tell I was an addict. They could smell it on me. And they could tell I was in trouble, so they wanted to protect me. Honestly, I was surprised how they took me in. Turns out they didn't like Five-five, and they told me Mr. Clean used to be a cop. They laughed about how I'd stolen the pills from them, almost like I was a hero. They stole shit all the time, everyone stealing shit from each other. I learned that nothing is really mine out here, except maybe my underwear. Some ho said to me once, 'Property is fluid.' Ain't that the truth."

Dylan scrunched up our napkins and stood up. He saluted the doughnut guy one more time and then held my hand. It was getting colder at night, and I planned to start carrying a blanket with me when I snuck out after that. I saw other people carrying blankets around their shoulders like capes. I imagined them as different superheroes: Purple Blanket Man, Mickey Mouse Blanket Man, Striped Blanket Man, Football Helmet Blanket Man, Plastic Blanket Man . . .

We found a lumpy soccer ball in a garbage can and took turns kicking it as we walked. Dylan could kick it farther than I could. I almost fell over whenever I kicked it, but it was funny and made me feel like I had a big brother. When we got to my building, Dylan looked like he was shaking as we stood there. I tried to think of a way I could let him sleep in my room when it turned colder outside.

"Maybe you shouldn't come out here anymore," he said. "It's pretty unsafe. I'm lucky to still be alive myself."

He looked up at the sky like he was looking for the moon. I searched too. Our breathing was silent.

"Your dad," he said. "He'll probably come back, but it will be when he's ready. And you might not recognize him. It could be a new dad or someone who feels like a dad. It doesn't really matter either way, as long as someone takes care of you. Family is . . . like . . . taking care of each other. You know, not even blood sometimes. Just taking care."

It sounded like he was about to say more but he didn't. I could tell he was thinking hard about something.

"When you're a teenager, and if I'm still around," he said, but then stopped. He leaned down and held out his hand for a handshake. "Let me teach you how to shake someone's hand," he said. His hand covered mine, and we moved our arms up and down. "Nice to meet you, sir," he said.

Our hands stayed connected like something else was supposed to happen. "Squeeze a little," he said.

So I did.

23

MOM AND BEN were on the couch having a discussion. That's what Mom called it when they talked about something they didn't really want to talk about. Their faces would get hard and they'd talk at the same time, and it was like when someone says yes and another person says no, and they discuss a problem louder and louder like a TV getting turned up. I didn't like it because it usually woke me up from a nap or sometimes, if it was at night, their discussions would sneak into my dreams.

One discussion about how Ben was an unsafe driver made me have a dream where Ben was driving us around in a tiny car and he kept hitting Stop signs and running over turtles. Later that day, I was trying to draw a picture of the dream for Tater, and even though it was messy and scribbly, he said he had a dream just like it, but with squirrels getting run over. Tater said dreams are weird pretend movies your brain makes up from all the stuff you've seen in your life. That's why, he said, people's eyeballs look like they're jumping around even when their eyes are closed. To see if this was true, I tried to look in a mirror when I was asleep once, but I don't think it worked. Or maybe it did but I was asleep and didn't wake up fast enough to see it happening.

Another discussion that turned into a dream was when

Mom said Ben wasn't giving me the right food to eat, and they talked about candy and popcorn for a long time, so I had a dream that I was crawling inside a giant piece of popcorn like it was a cave, but there was so much butter on it that I kept sliding out and I was covered in salt.

I heard discussions about a lot of things: how Ben didn't wear nicer clothes when they went out with friends, how Mom didn't like the right kind of music or movies, why Mom wouldn't give Ben her full heart.

Their discussion wasn't as loud as some of the other ones, but I could tell it was serious. Ben was talking about wanting to be a daddy and that I would be happier with a little brother or sister. Mom said maybe that was true but she wanted more time.

"What are you waiting for?" Ben said.

The way his voice came out when he said this was like the way my voice comes out when Mom tells me to stop whining. People's voices can sound a lot of ways—like inside normal voice, loud outdoor voice, library voice, plus mumbling, singing, and whining voices. People like whining the least, and it mostly makes people mad. There's a crying voice, too, but people feel sad when they hear that one.

"You know what I'm waiting for," Mom said.

"You need to move on," Ben said back.

"Maybe you're right," Mom said. "I think you're right. Maybe I need to move on."

"Hey, wait now," Ben said. "Don't make your life so hard. Be with me."

"It doesn't feel right, right now. It's not one hundred percent."

"And he feels one hundred percent to you? He's been gone since you came home from the hospital."

They were probably talking about Daddy. But I knew he

had seen me more than once. I knew he talked to me. I knew he was always there—or sometimes there, anyway. Maybe he wasn't the moon but something else up there. Maybe he was a star or something I couldn't see. I once heard someone say their dad was in a cloud called Heaven.

Neither of them said anything for a while. I could hear the sounds of the person who lived above us walking around their apartment. It was louder than anything coming from our place, and I didn't know if Mom and Ben were even still in the other room. Maybe they fell asleep. I got on the ground and crawled over to where I could see them on the couch. Mom was hugging Ben even though his arms were stiff by his legs, like he was trying to be a statue.

"I'm sorry," Mom said. "I should have told you."

They were whispering and I couldn't hear everything they were saying. Their faces were almost touching, and Mom kissed Ben under his eyes when he made a crying sound. She'd done this to me before, too, so my tears wouldn't touch the ground, she told me. Ben stood up and said he had to go to the bathroom. I crawled back to my room as fast as I could, before he had a chance to catch me spying. When he was done, I heard Mom zipping something up in the front room.

"That was fast," Ben said.

"This will be good for us, Ben. You'll see."

"Good for us, you mean, as a couple? Or good for us individually?"

"It'll be good for us," she said again.

"What if I don't want to take a break right now?" he asked.

"It's not all up to you," Mom said. "I really don't want to hurt you. You're important to me too."

I heard the front door open and the rolling wheels of a suitcase. "Here's your key," Ben said.

"And this one's yours," Mom said back.

"Worst trade ever," he said.

"I hope it doesn't have to be weird at work."

"Maybe I'll take some vacation time."

"That might be good. Where would you go?"

"Somewhere quiet probably. Do some soul searching. Look for myself."

Ben's words made me imagine him standing in a desert, turning in circles. How do you look for yourself? Aren't you already in yourself?

24

I GOT TO HAVE my first Halloween that year. The first one I could dress up for and get candy, anyway. Mom said we'd drive over to Tater's house because it was in a better neighborhood. I was confused, so she explained that our neighborhood didn't celebrate Halloween. She told me what trick-or-treating is and made me practice doing it. She closed her bedroom door and I knocked on it and waited for her to open it. She pretended to be surprised because I had a big pillowcase over my head like a ghost. I had to say "Trick or treat!" really loud, she told me, so the person answering the door would hear me. When we practiced doing it, I couldn't get the words right, though. I just said "treat" a bunch of times really fast. She told me to slow down, that it wasn't a race, and I should say *all three words*. I knocked on the door again, and when she answered, I said the word *trick* three times, really slow. When I finally did get all the words right, she said it sounded more like a question the way I said it: "Trick or treat?" I wanted to make sure I said it totally right so Mom would be proud and I could get enough treats to share with her.

As we drove to Tater's, it was getting dark and I saw other kids in their costumes. There were mummies and witches and robots and a fireman. There were a bunch of princesses and superhero cartoon guys and one grown-up dressed as a banana holding a baby, who was in a pineapple suit. I looked for Daddy in the sky but didn't see him. I wasn't sure if he would recognize me as a ghost, but I still hoped he would be out.

Tater said it was his first year of trick-or-treating, too, even though his parents had dressed him up before. His mom showed me a picture of him as a baby dressed as a pineapple. There must be a lot of pineapples that celebrate Halloween, I thought. In another picture, he was dressed up like a doll named Chuckie. This year he was wearing what looked like a torn-up fur coat and fake messed-up hair.

"This is my club," he said, showing me a big bone he was going to carry around.

I wasn't totally sure what he was supposed to be, even though I thought the bone was cool and wished I had one too.

"I'm a caveman, bro," he said.

"What's a caveman do?" I asked.

"I look for caves and kill things to eat," Tater said. "And also battle dinosaurs and bears. That's why I have this bear fur."

I tried to remember what ghosts do. I thought they ate pillows, but did they kill anything? Maybe birds.

We each carried plastic buckets with blinking lights attached so cars could see us in the dark. There were two holes cut in my ghost sheet for me to look out of. One of the holes was bigger than the other, so sometimes I had to grab it with my hand and put the holes where my eyes were so I could see where I was walking. Mom and Tater's mom were dressed up like tiger-striped cats, with fake whiskers and paws. They walked behind us, sometimes purring and laughing about their mom jokes, which usually had dirty words in them. I'm not sure why, but I could always tell when someone said a dirty word because it sounded different than the other words. Maybe because you can say a dirty word all by itself and you don't have to say anything else. You could say, "I fell down and hit my head," or just say the word *damnit*, and it's about the same thing. So when a grown-up said one word by itself, it was probably a dirty word and babies weren't supposed to say it. The word *shit* is a good example. You can say it when you drop something or forget something or run over something with your car, and even though you're mad, it's a fun word to say to make you feel better. Mom laughed when I said it once, even though I didn't know what it meant. *Fuck* is another word people say by itself a lot, but when I said it once, when we were at a baby store, nobody laughed, and everyone looked at me like I was a bad dog.

At one of the houses there was a werewolf wearing sunglasses and sitting on the porch, and scary sounds were coming from somewhere. I got scared and wanted to go to the next house instead.

"It's not real," Tater said. "Remember, it's for fun."

But it didn't *feel* fun and I didn't want to go to the door.

"Watch me," Tater said.

He walked up to where the werewolf was and poked it in the stomach. "His body's a pillow," he said. He knocked on the door and someone answered, slowly opening the door, barely enough to see Tater with his bucket.

"You're not a zombie, are you?" I heard the person ask Tater.

"No, I'm a caveman," Tater said.

"You could be a zombie, though. What's with the bone?"

"It's how I hunt for bears," Tater said.

The person reached their shaky hand out and dropped something in Tater's bucket. "Are you pro-zombie or anti-zombie?" they asked.

"Zombies are fake," Tater said.

"Well," the voice said, "I don't know about that. I'm a zombie hunter, and I killed one last week. It's buried under the porch, and I've been waiting for it to come back alive."

Tater backed away, and I could tell he was scared then too.

"Thank you for, um, the treat," he said, and then ran back to the sidewalk where we were all waiting for him. There were no other trick-or-treaters on our side of the street.

"That was intense," Tater said to us. "You gotta back me up next time, Tony." We heard the sounds from the house getting louder before it turned into a weird song, like a bunch of pianos rolling down a bumpy road. We suddenly saw a zombie crawl out from under the porch. We watched as it stood up and started to dance. It was so surprising that our moms screamed and then laughed until they got the hiccups.

Tater's mom took a bag of M&Ms out of his bucket and shared them with Mom.

"Everyone focuses on the candy, but the best part is dressing up," she said. "That's what you'll remember most. And seeing all the kids being scary and having fun outside at night."

I looked around in the sky again but still didn't see the moon. Not a sliver of Daddy's face anywhere. I thought maybe he was scared, but I saw other daddies walking around with their kids and they didn't seem to be scared. Some of them were even dressed up in costumes, like one guy who was a unicorn. Tater's dad was working in a forest somewhere and was gone for a few days, but at least Tater knew he was coming back. He said he was even going to save some Halloween candy for him.

We saw more zombies on the way back to Tater's house and I felt more scared of them than anything else.

"They only look frightening," Mom said. "But they're just silly make-believe."

"Even if they were real, they'd be too slow to catch us," Tater said. "And they bleed too much and they don't have brains, so they're dumb."

For a moment I forgot they weren't real, and I wondered if there were zombies who are dads and if their kids tried to help them get smarter. What would I do if I had a zombie dad?

"Why are they bleeding?" I asked.

"Because they pop their pimples too hard and they eat raw brains," Tater said.

That made me think of Dylan and how I saw him pop a pimple once and some blood came out. But I'd never heard of someone eating brains, unless they were a pig.

Mom said it was getting too late, so she picked me up and we all began walking back to Tater's. Over Mom's shoulder I saw someone walking behind us that had a droopy face. It was like the person I saw in the tall building once.

"Droopy," I said, and the person waved at me. They didn't have a bucket or a trick-or-treat bag. They walked behind us so quietly that no one else noticed. When we got to Tater's house, Droopy stopped walking and waved at me from under a streetlight.

At Tater's house, we dumped the candy out of our buckets and figured out what order we wanted to eat them in. Tater said he'd eat his gummy bears first because he was a caveman. I wanted to eat my candy corn first because I'd never had it before, and I like both candy and corn. Tater asked me what it tasted like and I said it tasted like the colors orange, white, and yellow all mixed together.

Mom and Tater's mom told us to go to bed, but we didn't want to fall asleep yet. We got under the covers on his bed but were secretly playing with building blocks while our moms had their mom time, as they called it.

"This is our underground city," Tater said. He told me the rules of the underground city, like where kids were allowed to play and what part of the city the bad guys lived in. "Some of the bad guys are zombies," he said, "and they're not allowed in restaurants."

We heard our moms laughing about something in the other room, and we tried to listen in to see what was so funny.

"Close your eyes and you can hear better," Tater said. "Our ears can be spies."

I heard them talking about someone having a baby and that they didn't know who the daddy was, but they said "baby daddy," and it was the first time I'd heard of a baby being a daddy, but it seemed to make sense because I had seen some babies who were very large, and sometimes kids have fake babies they practice being moms and dads with. I wondered if I would be a baby daddy someday.

Then Tater's mom was talking about Tater, and I heard her say he "can be a real son of a bitch." It didn't sound nice, but Mom laughed really loud about it. I looked at Tater to see if he was hearing them, but his mouth had drool coming out of it and he looked asleep.

I wasn't sure if we were having a sleepover, but I wasn't sleepy yet. I got out of his bed and looked out the window. I wondered if there were still trick-or-treaters outside. I didn't see any, but I did see Droopy still out there, under the light. They looked at me and waved. I thought I could see a smile on their droopy face. They walked to the window and the light stayed on them, like it was attached to their body somehow. I couldn't tell if they were a man or a woman or a kid. The droopy mouth was moving, saying something, but I couldn't hear it through the window. They moved closer and touched the glass. I heard the creaking sound of the window going up.

It only opened a little bit and Droopy put their mouth by the open part.

"Can you hear me?" they said.

I nodded.

"I sent you a fax," they said.

"I can't read," I said.

"You can read this one," they said. "I sent it tonight."

"What does it say?"

"You'll see. You'll understand."

"Who are you?"

"I am the one who knows everything. I'm sorry this is happening."

I looked up above Droopy's head and saw that the light was coming from a low moon in the sky. I heard the jingle of car keys and then Mom's voice coming into the room.

"What the heck are you doing?" she said. "Are you aiming to run away again?"

Tater's mom was next to her, laughing, with her hand over her mouth.

"Droopy," I said.

"What?" said Mom.

"Droopy," I said again, and looked at the window. Nothing was there but the darkness of outside.

"You have to go to the bathroom?" she asked me.

I put my hands on my face and tried to pull my skin down to make it look droopy.

"Okay," she said. "Let's go home then. You're going to give Tater nightmares making faces like that."

I looked at Tater and could see he was awake. His eyes were open, staring at me.

25

IT WAS A DRAWING of the moon and its moonbeam. Inside the lines of the moonbeam, a drawing of a gun. There was the shape of someone lying down close to the gun. Two stick lines for legs, two for the arms, one line for the body, and a circle for the head. It came from the fax machine. It made me think of the show my babysitter was watching on TV that first night I went out to look for Daddy. The gun, the alleyway, the dumpster, the police cars. But there were no cars or dumpster in this picture.

I looked at it closely and even though it looked like something another little kid could have drawn with a marker, I knew that it was from Droopy because they said they'd sent it. And Droopy said they knew everything. I could imagine Droopy drawing the picture and pushing the buttons on another fax machine to send it to me. Holding the picture in my hands made it feel real. I wondered if everything the fax machine told me was going to be true, and if it was, I'd have to go out and find the story it was trying to tell me. Maybe at the end of the story I would find Daddy and the world could finally feel right and normal.

I just wanted everything to be normal.

I went out the next night after Mom had gone to bed early.

She said she felt sick, probably because she ate all of my Reese's peanut butter cups. The light outside looked strange, and when I looked at the sky, I saw something I'd never seen before: three moons at the same time. I thought one was a pig pretending to be Daddy. Another one was bleeding onto a cloud under it. And the one I thought was Daddy looked different, like it was shrinking. I was not going to be fooled by the false moons, though. Mom had warned me. She said, "On the night after Halloween, all the ghosts and ghouls disappear into thin air until the next year." And I knew when things disappeared, they floated up to the sky. Usually people couldn't see the disappearing thing, but I must be special because there are things that I see that no one else seems to notice. Dr. Duck-Duck said I was special, too, because I heard her say to Mom that I was a special kind of special.

I was holding the picture from Droopy to show Daddy. I hoped it was a secret message for Daddy that meant he was coming home. I was wearing pajamas that made me look like a little bear. Mom called them my fuzz-butt PJs, and they even covered my feet. There was a hood, too, if I wanted to cover my head. It felt like I was wearing a teddy bear.

There weren't as many sidewalk people as usual, and it was colder outside. I looked up at the three moons. The one with the pig face glowed brighter when I held up the picture.

"Do you know where this is?" I said as loud as possible.

"What's that you got now?" said a woman behind me.

Her voice startled me, and I dropped the paper in a puddle of something on the sidewalk. She looked familiar and her eyes squinted down at me. "You're the one they call Timmy, right?"

"Tony," I said. I couldn't be sure though. Maybe they called me Timmy out here and I didn't know it.

"I'm trying to remember who you belong to," she said. "Someone at Banjo's, wasn't it?"

I remembered her voice. She was the one who took me to the Mexican food place that night when I ate the cheese quesadilla. "La-La quesadilla," I said.

"You call me whatever you like, baby," she said, "but don't call me Momma."

La-La bent down to grab the fax machine message. She picked it up like a dirty sock and frowned. She turned it sideways and upside down, and then blew on it. "You draw this?" she asked.

"It's from Droopy," I said.

"Droopy? Who's Droopy? You talkin' about that bitch who smokes crack out of a corncob pipe?"

"Droopy," I said again. "The one with the face."

She smelled the paper and looked at me. "This is messed up," she said, pointing at the drawing. "Is this supposed to be a UFO?"

I pointed to the sky. "The moon," I said.

La-La looked up, and I did too. The moon that looked like a pig face was gone. The real moon was there, but it looked too small and its light twitched like it was trying to stay awake. The bleeding moon was still up there too, dripping on the cloud underneath it. It looked like it was shining a red glow on something down the street from us.

"This ain't right," La-La said. She looked nervous. She was about to say something else but a loud sound, like a bomb, suddenly shook the air around us. She fell to her knees and grabbed me, covering me like a shield. She was wearing a long black, slick coat, and she gathered me up in it. I was too scared to do anything, so I tried to make myself as light as possible so she could run away faster. I thought of myself as a small toy,

137

like a teddy bear or my light-up Ray bat. La-La was fast and strong, like a superhero.

She ran around a corner, between some cars with broken windows, behind a mini-mart, through someone's driveway, into a backyard, and back out onto a street. There were old brick buildings with graffiti sprayed all over them, flickering streetlights, and trash cans overflowing. She stopped and listened. I was pressed against her, inside her slippery coat, with my head peeking out. I smelled something smoky, and I waited for the next explosion or scream or some other sound, but it was quiet. I didn't see anyone else around. It reminded me of the time I heard Mom tell Ben about a dream where she was the last person alive and she just walked around, looking for anyone else still alive.

I looked in the sky but couldn't find Daddy anymore. The bleeding moon was still there, though, and we were standing near its glow. The cloud that was catching its red drip was gone, but there was a light coming out of the bleeding moon. It was like a red spotlight pointing to something in the alleyway. It looked like there was a body or a stick figure on the ground. La-La put me down and turned me away from it so I couldn't see. She walked toward it slowly.

"Don't look," she said, but I was already looking. It was like the picture from the fax machine.

Droopy must have wanted me to see. He thought I needed to know.

It was Dylan, lit up in red, on the ground.

"Don't look," La-La said again. But I kept looking.

"You shouldn't see this," she said.

I stepped closer. La-La leaned over and grabbed Dylan's shoulders and shook them like she was mad at him. I didn't know what to say, but I tapped his knee and then kicked his legs to see if he would wake up. I kept kicking and nothing happened. I thought of Dr. Duck-Duck and the way my leg kicked when she tapped my knee. *Bonk bonk!*

"Is he sleeping?" I asked La-La. She didn't say anything. The strange moon was right above us, watching us, dripping red light.

"Yes," she said. "Leave him be."

"Where is everyone?" I asked.

She picked me up again and held me even tighter.

"I'm going to take you back to the neighborhood, and you're going to show me where you live," she said. As we walked, the light of the red moon faded, and then the sky looked totally dark. All was quiet except La-La's teeth chattering. It sounded like a wind-up toy I saw once—clicking teeth opening and closing really fast and skipping across a table.

We walked for a long time, and then she finally asked me, "Is that boy really your family?"

I remembered when Dylan told her we were cousins, but I wasn't sure if it was true. "Yes," I said, hoping she wouldn't ask more questions.

"You shouldn't say anything to your mom and dad about this. And you should stay in your home when it's dark outside. You're lucky no one kidnaps you or calls the pigs on you."

I was nervous for a moment that La-La was going to kidnap me or call the pigs. I'd heard stories about kidnapping, and I thought it had something to do with naptime but in places you shouldn't nap. "Stranger danger" is what they called it. But I liked strangers. They were some of my favorite people.

We were close to my apartment, but I didn't want her to know where I lived. We walked by a place that used to be a Burger King. I saw an empty sleeping bag in front, and the door had a big piece of wood in it where there used to be glass. We walked past it, but then La-La turned around and went back.

"Shit," she said, and put me down. "Stay here. I'll be right back."

She pulled the door and it opened just enough for her to slip inside. I remembered being there with Mom when I was two years old, eating french fries. She even ordered a milkshake to dip them in. Maybe La-La was seeing if there were any french fries in there. I waited for a while and started feeling cold. I went to the door and pulled on it, to see if I could look at what was inside. It was hard to hold it open, but there wasn't much to see anyway. There was a small light in one corner—maybe a flashlight or a small fire. I thought about saying hello into the dark, but I was afraid it would echo. I got a weird feeling in my stomach, so I closed the door and walked away fast. I looked around to make sure I was going the right way.

A light flickered on me and then grew into a bright white circle. It was Daddy, coming out from behind a cloud. I wondered how long he'd been up there. Maybe he was watching to see that I made it home safe. His moonlight pointed me the right way and then followed me while I walked.

"Where have you been?" I asked.

"I had something important I had to do," he said. His face was full and large. His mouth, or what I think was his mouth, stayed open in a circle. One of his eyes was dark and the other shiny.

"There were other moons I hadn't seen before tonight," I said. "Do you know them?"

"Sometimes there are strange moons, but not everyone can see them. Did you see them with your eyes, Tony?"

"Yes, but they went away. I'm not sure where."

We got close to home and I slowed down, hoping we could talk more. I still didn't see anyone else out. The sidewalks were bare. I heard a low *whooshing* sound that I think was Daddy's breathing.

"How is your mother?" he asked me.

"She's fine," I said.

I felt myself getting angry for some reason. I didn't know what to say. I looked for something to stare at so I wouldn't lose my temper.

"She's the best mother in the world," he said. "Always stay near her. Cherish her strength and let it become part of you. You can trust her and be sure of her heart. Listen to her always and know that what she gives you is constant love. What she gives you is always enough."

I started to tune him out. The words all sounded the same. How would he know anything about her?

"Shut up," I said.

Silence.

Silence.

Silence.

He tried to whisper. "Why do you want me to—"

"It's *not* enough! You're not here. I don't even know if you've ever held me or made food for me or pushed me in a stroller or played peekaboo with me. If you have, I don't remember it. I mean, why are you a moon when every other dad is a real person? I could be home sleeping instead of trying to find you."

"But your mom told you this is what I am," he said.

I thought about that and all the stories I'd been told. When grown-ups say things to their babies, they should be true. They shouldn't be like a fairy tale or some kind of wish that doesn't come true. I knew I wasn't the only person who talked to the moon, but I still felt alone.

"Do you know any other dads that are like you?" I asked.

"Every father is different," he said.

That made me remember the first time I saw it snowing outside. Mom said that every snowflake is different, even though they all looked the same to me and they all piled up to make the outside look like it was covered with a clean white carpet that looked the same everywhere I could see. After that, one snowflake always looked like the next snowflake, even on TV. So that story about all snowflakes being different was probably never true. They were all the same, like daddies should all be the same.

"Maybe I should find a new daddy," I said. "One that's not a moon."

The moon did not answer. The breathing sound changed. It sounded like wind. I heard the sound of a bell coming from somewhere. It sounded like my apple bell. I wanted to go home and play with my apple bell. I wanted to talk to it like I talked to Dylan and Daddy.

I kept my head down as I walked the last few steps to home. I knew the moon was still there because it lit my path, but I didn't care. I looked down and quietly made my way back inside.

Before I got in bed, I saw there was a new note from the fax machine. This one had letters from the alphabet. Words. I folded it up and put it in a secret hiding spot by my coloring books.

I let my mind imagine that the note said something good. I pretended it was a story about a moon that's just a moon and a mom who is happy and a dad who sleeps in a bed and wakes up laughing because his son starts bouncing on the bed. The boy laughs, too, and bounces so much he can touch the ceiling. The sun comes in through the window, and everyone in the house is happy because they slept all night long through the darkness and their dreams were good.

FOUR YEARS OLD

26

"YOU'RE GETTING so tall," Mom said. She kept looking down at me and smiling as we walked to the grocery store. "I could have sworn you were only up to my knee last week. Now you're like, I don't know, a giraffe or something."

She was in a happy mood but acting funny, like she was going to play a trick on me. Her voice changed and got kind of squeaky and high like a cartoon when she was like this and it made me nervous.

Grown-ups are good at acting this way when they want to fool someone. They act too nice and then they secretly do something that's not very nice. A lot of people don't seem to know this is a trick, but I can always tell. Little kids try to do this trick, too, but it only works sometimes. Grown-ups usually know something's up when kids act too nice. I have no idea what happens if a grown-up and a kid are doing this trick at the same time. Does only one trick work or can both of them work, so you end up with two people fooled?

"You're tall, too, Mom," I said.

She laughed and put her hand above her head like she was measuring herself. "I guess it runs in the family."

I tried to think of other nice things to say. "You're like a pretty giraffe," I said.

She laughed harder. "Are you just repeating everything I say here?"

"Are you repeating everything here to say?"

"You little wise-butt!"

"You little wise-butt!"

"I feel like pooping my pants."

"I feel like poo—." I couldn't say it all back. I laughed too hard whenever anyone said "pooping."

"Are you trying to butter me up so I'll get you a cookie at the store?" she asked.

I didn't even know why I was trying to play the acting-too-nice trick on her. Usually it *was* because I wanted a cookie or a new toy. The last time I did it she bought me a pretend vacuum cleaner I wanted to play with. But this time I guess I was just playing a joke to make her smile. I kept going and tried to have a serious look on my face. "Are you trying to get a butter cookie at the store?"

"Supercalifragilisticexpialidocious."

"Super . . . cow . . . fraggle . . . suss."

"Ha!" Mom said. "I gotcha on that one."

"You made it up," I said.

"It's a real word," she said. "We can look it up when we get home. There's even a song."

I got to sit inside the shopping cart at the store—not the baby part, but the big part where all the groceries go. I used to sit in that little part, though, and sometimes Mom would grab my feet and steer that way. It was pretty funny back then.

My job in the shopping cart was to guard our groceries so Mom could concentrate on her list. She bought vegetables, eggs, some cans of something with a fish on it, a jar with a cartoon bee on it, a bottle of red stuff, a bottle of green gross-looking stuff, and a box of things she said were only for her. "Moms only," she said. I touched the box against my nose.

146

It didn't smell like a snack, so I didn't really care.

We went to the cold part of the store last. She put a bag of frozen peas on my head and said, "Here's your new hat."

I let it sit there and pretended to like it. This is another way to play a trick on someone: pretend their trick is normal and fine and it happens every day and there's nothing to laugh about. If nobody laughs, it means the trick did not work.

"I like my hat," I said.

"That's good," she said. "Maybe I can wear it sometime."

"It's mine," I said. The bag slid off my head and plopped into my lap.

"Oh, hey, look over there!" she said, pointing to some bags of ice. When I looked, I knew she was grabbing something and hiding it behind her back.

"What?" I said.

"Look at those bags of ice. I wish I knew how they keep from melting."

She was trying to distract me, and I fell for it and started thinking about all the things that make ice melt: fire, water, sand, belly buttons, sharks, parking lots. And if you put ice inside a TV, it would probably melt there too.

"That's my hat," I said to the cashier when he scanned the frozen peas and added up our stuff. He looked at me like I was crazy. Strangers are so serious sometimes.

When we got outside, Mom reached into the bag and said, "Wanna see magic?"

I nodded. She pulled two ice-cream sandwiches out of the bag and gave me one. We sat at a picnic table by the side of the store and Mom unwrapped our treats. Even though Mom called them ice-cream sandwiches, I noticed they weren't made of bread. It was ice cream and these two things shaped like bread that tasted kind of like cake.

"Do you know what today is, Tony?"

I was mostly concentrating on my ice cream, so I didn't say anything.

"Are you listening?"

I was trying to find a part of the ice-cream sandwich that wasn't too cold for my teeth. I bit one of the corners and said, "Uh-huh."

"It's my birthday. The day I was born. Can you guess how old I am?"

I'd never looked at Mom and thought she was any age. I always thought you stopped counting when you grow up. I was getting better at counting, but I still wasn't very good at it yet.

"Thirteen?" I said.

"Uh, no," she said.

"One million?" I said.

"Not quite," she said. "I'm twenty-five years old. I was born in a hospital about six blocks that way. Like you, I was in my mother's belly for eight and a half months before I was born. Decided to check out the world a little early, I guess. Not sure why we were in such a hurry, but here we are. Every single day counts, right?"

I'd never heard Mom talk about herself as a baby before, and when others mentioned her mom and dad, not much was said. I didn't even know that grandmothers and grandfathers were the parents of moms and dads. I didn't think I had any grandmothers or grandfathers.

"My mother was a little older than me when she had her first baby," she said. "She was thirty-two when your aunt Maria was born and thirty-five when I was born. My father was seven years younger than her. He disappeared when I was little. I don't have any memories of him, but my mother said he loved me very much. I never found out what happened to him. I think she was going to tell me when I got older, but she got really sick when I was in fifth grade and talking got hard for her."

"Was she throwing up?" I asked.

"Not sick like that. It was something in her brain. But we didn't have much help. I took turns with Maria taking care of her. Maria had the same father as I did, and she could remember a few things about him, but she didn't know what happened to him either."

An old man outside the store saw us and walked over. "Hey, Jennie," he said, like he knew her.

"Oh, hey there," Mom said back.

"I heard it's your birthday today. I hope you're taking the day off to do something fun," he said.

"Well, yes, it is, and yes, I am," she said. "I got some good company and some ice cream. What more could I want?"

The man smiled and nodded at me. "Treat your momma extra nice today," he said before walking into the store. I knew he wasn't Mom's dad, but he seemed like someone's dad.

"I don't remember that dude's name," Mom said. "He comes into Crown sometimes and buys old movies on videotape and says I should watch one with him. Kind of a creeper. Hits on everyone though, so maybe I'm not the only one."

"Hitting is bad," I said.

"I didn't mean that," she said. "I shouldn't have said it that way. I mean, like . . . have you ever seen someone who just wants to kiss everybody?"

"Gross," I said. It was a word I didn't say a lot but it seemed to describe a lot of things in the world, like kissing.

"Anyway, what were we talking about?"

"Daddy."

"Daddy? Oh, *my* dad," she said. "Yeah, so many dads are the great mysteries of the world. You'd have better luck finding a Sasquatch."

It seemed like telling me about her parents was making her a little sad, but she was also laughing and making up funny jokes. It's kind of the way she always was, really, like she had to cry before she could laugh.

"I always thought my father would come back, even after my mother was gone."

"Where did she go?" I asked.

"Oh. Well, she went to Heaven the summer before I went into sixth grade. Her name was Angelica, but people called her Angel, believe it or not."

She looked into the sky like she might find an angel or figure out where Heaven was. She took a bite of her ice-cream sandwich. "Birth and death and ice cream," she said.

I wasn't totally sure how death worked. If people went to Heaven or the moon or got buried in a coffin, were they really dead? Weren't they still there? Does dead just mean people can't talk to you anymore?

"Maria and I moved in with another family down the street. They basically adopted us, and they had a lot of kids already. They were hippies, so they had funny names. I mean, the parents were named Bob and Mary, but the kids were called Ocean and Sun and Energy. Maria was best friends with Ocean. Energy and I were friends, but we also hated each other sometimes. Sun was this cute little Asian boy, probably five years old. I think he was adopted too. A few other kids came and went, but I can't remember their names. One summer there was a kid named Harold who lived there, and I was so used to the hippie names that *Harold* seemed like the funniest name ever. Anyway, I still thought I'd meet my father someday. I imagined him to look like a high-school quarterback for some reason. Like Prince Valiant."

"Prince who?"

"Prince Valiant. He's a dude from an old comic strip with a

cool haircut. I thought he was kind of hot, but I never really understood the story."

"Your dad was a prince?"

"Oh, I don't know what he was, Tony. I had these kooky fantasies about him. I played softball for a couple of years, and I always hoped I would see him in the bleachers. If I missed a bus somewhere, I thought he would drive up and ask me if I needed a ride. When I tried to sing in a band once, I thought if I became famous, he'd show up at a concert and he would say he was proud of me. Stuff like that. After a while I got used to it only being a fantasy. Even losing can start to feel okay if you don't think you'll ever win."

I realized then that Mom and I both had dads that were secret. We just had to figure out what the secrets were. Her dad was a comic strip and mine was the moon. But how did that happen?

"Did you ever win?" I asked her.

"Yeah," she said. "In some ways, I've won a lot. But you can't win all the time because nobody's perfect. And that's what makes the winning parts better: knowing you found a way to get yourself through."

We finished the ice-cream sandwiches and sat at the picnic table for a while longer. Mom gave me a new toy she found for me at her work. It was a blue guy with big muscles and a skeleton face. "I got it for you a while ago," she said, "but I thought it might be too scary. Someone said it's probably collectible. His face is made out of real bone. Pretty weird, but cool, I guess."

"It's not too scary," I said. I touched the bone face and thought about how glad I was not to have a cast on my arm anymore. The skeleton face looked like it was laughing. I imagined him saying something like, "You will never defeat me!"

"What's 'collectible'?" I asked.

She picked it up and looked at it closer. "Collectible is

when there's not many made of something. Like, instead of a million, there's a hundred. Look at his foot. There's a word in some other language. Maybe Russian."

"What's Russian?" I said.

"It's something from Russia, which is another country really far away. You can't even see it, it's so far away."

I wondered if Russia was a place where Daddy went. Was it a place where dead things go? Maybe there were a lot of bones there—enough to make a collectible skeleton man. A hundred bones sounded like it was bigger than a whole mountain.

"See how fun mom birthdays are?" she said. "You got ice cream, and a sad story from memory lane, and an action figure that's probably worth a million dollars. And you didn't have to get me anything. No one had to get me anything."

"I got you something," Skeleton Face said. But it was really me, holding up the toy and changing my voice.

Mom smiled and laughed. The sun got brighter on her face. I looked at her nose, her teeth, her chin. Her eyes looked like wishes. Her hand touched my hand. She leaned over and kissed Skeleton Face, part of her lips on his real bone and part of her lips on my hand. My heart wanted to say "I love you" to her brain.

"What did you get me?" she asked.

Skeleton Face said, "I got you, um—" but I didn't know what to say.

"I got you too," she said to him. Then she smushed my face and kissed me a hundred times. "I got you, Tony Volcano!" She turned it into a song. "I got you, babe . . . I got you, babe . . . I got yoooou, babe."

27

AUNT MARIA WAS making dinner for Mom for her birthday. She even came over with a special machine called a Crock-Pot to make a casserole. There was also cake for dessert and tequila, which was in a bottle that had a picture of a skeleton wearing a hat riding on a chicken. They said I couldn't have any of the tequila, so they gave me water instead. They poured really small baby sips of the tequila into tiny glasses for themselves, and they let me drink my water out of a tiny glass too. They said, "To your health!" and "Down the hatch!" and then we all touched our glasses together and swallowed really fast. They made sour faces when they swallowed, and then a funny sound came out of them. Sometimes they burped without making a sound. They let me smell the tequila, acting like it was something I should be scared of. It smelled like a chicken covered in Band-Aids, which was probably what the picture on the bottle meant. Maybe it had real skeleton in it too. It smelled terrible, but I liked the way they drank it, like it was some kind of game.

I played with my train set as they made dinner. All the tracks were made of wood that connected together. Some of them were curves and some of them were straight parts. A couple of tracks were like hills, and there were other parts that weren't tracks at all—like tunnels and pretend trees and pretend buildings.

I knew that in real life trains had to go through mountains and woods and sometimes they went through cities. When they went through cities, the trains had to be careful not to crash into things, like dogs or gas stations. I kept rearranging the parts, so sometimes it was a big circle or sometimes it didn't all connect and there was a dead end. When there was a dead end, the train had to go backwards, but it still worked. I would pretend I was on one of the trains with Dylan and we were going to a zoo to look at animals. I had a lot of animals standing next to each other on the other side of a red bridge that went up and down. The train could only go to the zoo when the bridge was down. There were horses, monkeys, some tigers, a dolphin, and a giant squirrel. Sometimes the squirrel, whose name was Kenny, rode on the dolphin's back. I had been to three different zoos in my life, but this one would have been the best one if it were real.

Mom and Maria were in the kitchen talking about when they were kids. I listened in, hoping they'd tell some funny secrets. Like, I wondered if they ever snuck out at night to look for their dad—a prince or quarterback. They were making a lot of cooking noises with big spoons and knives in there, but that usually meant they were having fun. Maria didn't have a baby yet, but she said she would someday. She was married to a man who worked in a factory. His name was Jay, and he turned on the machines that made ketchup and stuff like that. A ketchup man, they always said. I thought about what it would be like to become a ketchup man when I grew up.

During dinner they drank more tiny glasses of tequila. The casserole was so good because there was a lot of cheese, and the soft beans and rice mushed together perfectly so I could eat it with my Elmo spoon instead of a fork. Forks made me feel nervous when I tried to use them because I poked myself in the cheek once and decided I didn't want to use one again unless I really had to.

"It's almost bedtime, Tony," Mom said, "but I'll let you have some of my birthday cake first if you do the Roadrunner dance with me."

I wanted cake so I let her pick me up. She pushed a button on her computer that made music come out of a little speaker. A guy with a funny voice started a song by counting to six and then some drums and a clangy guitar sound jumped out of the speaker at the same time. Mom held me up with one arm and did the dance move where she shrugged one of her shoulders up and then the other one and bounced a little on her feet too. She looked at each shoulder as she shrugged them, and her face made her look like she was pooping.

The funny-voice guy sang about being in love with moonlight and the radio and being out at night. I bounced along to the drums and Mom was cracking up and having a hard time holding me. She let me down and danced in front of me and I tried to do the same moves as her, like Simon Says. Maria was watching us and pretending to play guitar with one of those things you flip pancakes with.

There was a part in the middle of the song where the music stopped really quick and the singer said, "I'm in love with rock and roll and I'll be out all night," and Mom and Maria sang it, too, and then the song kept going. When this happened, it was called a dance party, and it was fun but also kind of embarrassing because I'd never had dance lessons.

There was a loud knock at the door, and we all stopped and turned down the music. We tried to be totally silent like when you play hide-and-seek, but we couldn't help laughing. There was another knock, but this time it was a little quieter, like someone being shy.

"Okay, okay," Mom said. "Get the cake ready. We might need to make peace."

Mom tiptoed to the door and looked through the peephole to see who it was. "Shit," she said.

"Jennie?" the knocking person said.

Maria walked over and looked through the peephole too. "Jesus," she said.

The person knocked again, and Maria said, "We don't want any!"

"Let me just give you your birthday present."

"You should have texted me before you came over," Mom said. "How did you get in? This is unacceptable."

"It'll only be one minute."

Mom told me to go to my room, and I did, but only so I could grab a blanket to hide under in the hallway. Maria looked over but didn't see me spying. She nodded at Mom and said, "I'm right here. Let's get this over with."

Mom opened the door, and Ben stood there with some flowers and a present wrapped in a silver box. "Hey," he said.

"Ben, I already told you I didn't want you to get me a present this year, and you know why."

"It's just something I saw and decided to buy for you. It wasn't premeditated."

"That's still a present, Ben."

Maria stepped between them and took the box from Ben. "She said she needs space," she told him. "You can't *make* her commit to you. Don't you want her to think deeply about this so she can be confident and happy in whatever she decides?"

Ben stepped back and threw up his hands like someone who doesn't know the right answer to a question. "Yes, of course I want that," he said. "But it's driving me crazy. I think I should be able to argue my case."

"Argue your case?" Mom said.

"I just miss you," he said.

"Well, just don't then," Mom said.

"Hey, hey, hey!" Maria said. "That's enough talking for tonight. This is a good example of why you two need more time."

Then Ben said something that made me both confused and happy. It made me think he could be a daddy someday for someone. And this whole time I'd been afraid that he was going to take Mom away from me when maybe he wasn't. He said, "I miss Tony too."

It turned quiet after he said this. I stuck my head out from under the blanket and looked at them all, standing there like statues, staring at each other. It was like time had stopped and I held my breath, waiting for more. A thought was turning into a picture in my head: Ben standing tall and smiling, holding a baby and feeding it with a baby bottle. And in this thought, the baby was happy! But it was a baby who didn't mind that his dad is pushy and liked dumb jokes.

"It's hard for me to sit and wait around," Ben said. His voice sounded crinkly. "We talked about things, about doing stuff. I started to think into the future too much, probably. But I couldn't help it, and I still can't help it. And I'm going to be really sad if we suddenly stop . . . if our togetherness stops."

He walked over to the table where some of the food was, like he was going to spoon up some casserole and make himself at home. He picked up a napkin instead and blew his nose in it. He looked over and saw me hiding but didn't say anything. He didn't give me away.

"I like looking forward to things," he said in my direction before turning back to Mom. "Do you remember when that cool art couple wanted to make us dinner? The ones who bought all that vintage furniture from us, like twenty couches and chairs? It was a month's worth of sales in one day. They invited us to their house for a meal, and we were both super excited. I put it in my mental calendar, and I thought about it a few times—how cool that night was going to be. But we never made it happen. It's something I still think about doing, though, even though we probably never will."

"I remember them," Mom said. "I didn't think they were serious, though."

"You never think anyone's serious," Ben said. "It's like you don't believe in people."

"Why should I?" Mom said. But she didn't say this like she was asking a question. She said it like she was scared. Like she was pointing a knife at someone in front of her.

"I can count on one hand how many people I trust, and when it comes to people who've let me down, I've lost count," she said. "I know you want to be a good thing for me, Ben, but I've had people disappear all over the place on me, and you can't really understand what my life has been like because of that. And I get exhausted even thinking about how much time it would take to tell you all the stories."

Mom grabbed a napkin and blew her nose too. She poured tequila into her tiny glass and held it up in front of her.

"I'm twenty-five," she said. "But sometimes I feel like I'm a hundred and five. Here's to getting older and to those who got lost along the way." She drank the tequila and then almost fell down trying to sit in her chair.

"Can I have some of that?" Ben asked.

"No," Mom said. "Not yet."

Maria pulled Ben over to the door and opened it. "Okay, you guys had a little talk and that's good, but that's as far as we get tonight. Time to say good night."

Ben lowered his head and went out the door.

Mom watched through the peephole to make sure he walked away. She and Maria held hands and started whisper-talking about something. I thought about calling out, to see if I could come out and have a piece of cake, but Mom looked mad so I thought I should stay hidden and quiet. They both looked at the silver box on the table. It was the size of a shoebox and had a white ribbon wrapped around it.

"What do you think it is?" Maria said.

"I don't know. Hopefully a six-pack of pepper spray."

"Or a Taser?"

"That would be thoughtful at least."

Mom picked up the box and shook it. I wanted to shake it, too, but I was still hiding. I hoped it was something fun like a game or a train. Mom cut the ribbon and opened the box. There was a bunch of crumpled up paper in different colors, and Mom took them out of the box. I wondered why Ben gave her a box of thrown-away paper, but maybe he didn't know how to fold paper well and there were notes written on them or pictures he drew for her. Mom didn't bother to look at them. She pulled out another box from inside the box. She unwrapped it and there was another box. And another box inside that one. The last box was black and tiny, about the size of a baby hand. I wanted to know why Ben had wasted those other boxes when he could have just given her the last one.

"Oh my God," Maria said. "What the hell?"

They both stared at the box without opening it. Maria was shaking her hands in the air and Mom looked like she was trying to pull her hair out. I wasn't sure why they were freaking out about it. I knew about freaking out because Tater always said it when he got super excited. He'd say things like, "Sorry about freaking out," or "I'm freaking out!"

Maybe there was something bad in the box, like a spider or a shrunken head. I saw a shrunken head once, and it was the scariest thing ever.

"Can you open it, Maria?" Mom asked.

"I think this is something you have to face yourself."

I wanted to open the box myself and get it over with, but I could only watch.

Mom held the box in front of her and opened it slowly. She looked shaky, like she might fall down. Maria moved closer and put her arm around Mom to look too. Mom closed the box and Maria said, "Well, that happened."

I wanted to know what was inside the box, but I decided to crawl back to my room. I had my blanket over me, with my head sticking out like a turtle. I counted in my head as high as I could to make time pass faster. I waited for one of them to call my name and give me cake.

"Mommmm!" I finally called out.

She walked into my room and found me on the floor under my blanket. "Didn't you fall asleep yet, you little groundhog?" She picked me up and put me in bed. She tucked the blanket all around my body and it felt like I was wrapped in a burrito.

"Cake, please," I said.

"Oh, Tony. I can't put anything else in my stomach tonight. We'll have some for lunch dessert tomorrow. Deal?"

"Okay."

Maria poked her head in the room and asked if she could sleep on the couch. Mom smiled and gave her the thumbs-up sign. "Good night, burrito baby," Maria said.

"Good night, couch," I said back.

Mom rubbed my head and I was so tired I couldn't keep my eyes open. Sometimes when she put me to bed, she accidentally fell asleep too. I liked when she slept next to me because it felt like we were two floating feathers with nothing but darkness and air around us.

28

TATER WANTED to explain Thanksgiving to me as our moms did something to a turkey in the kitchen. We were at Tater's house and Tater's dad sat with us in the living room. There was a parade on TV and some giant cartoon balloons were being pulled on strings through the air. Tater's dad was reading something on his computer and sometimes looked up when we asked him who some of the cartoon balloons were.

"That's Smokey Bear," he said about a friendly-looking bear wearing a hat. "And that's the guy from *The Nutcracker*," he said about another balloon. "I don't know who that one is," he said about a superhero in a cool red suit.

"His name is Red Power Ranger, Dad," Tater said.

Maria was coming over for Thanksgiving dinner later and so were some of Tater's cousins. It was getting colder outside, so people wore big coats when they went outdoors, and Mom told us it might even snow soon. The last time it snowed there was a car parked by our apartment and it had snow all over its roof and bumpers. Mom took me outside to look at it, and we put our hands in the snow and made a small snowman we named Pie. We went outside a few times to see Pie, standing proudly on that car like Santa Claus riding on his sleigh. Then one day he melted down into a wet white lump with a carrot on top. And then the next day the car was gone, and we never saw it again.

I hadn't snuck out since the time I saw Droopy and La-La. The night when there were three moons and I saw Dylan on the ground. But I could still see the Daddy moon sometimes when it was in the sky during the day, and I would wave to it at night through my window. Mom put some plastic stuff over my window, she said to save on bills, but I didn't like it because what if Daddy said something and I couldn't hear it?

"Thanksgiving is the day when we celebrate all the turkeys in America," Tater said to me. "And we thank them for letting us eat them."

"And what can you tell us about Christopher Columbus?" Tater's dad said.

Tater made a face at his dad like he wasn't supposed to interrupt but then looked like he remembered something.

"Oh yeah," he said. "Christopher Crumpets discovered all the turkeys, and then the cowboys and Indians killed them all for a feast. Do you know what cranberry sauce is?"

I shook my head.

"It's the turkey blood."

"Tater!" his dad said. "That's not true. Cranberry sauce is made from fruit, and it's delicious."

When we ate that night, I didn't want any cranberry sauce on my plate. I had orange potatoes, carrots, a roll, and one piece of turkey. I didn't know any of Tater's cousins or remember any of their names. I thought of them in my head as Red Shirt, Funny Guy, Tall Lady, Coughing Man, Carpet Hair, Bald Head, Smiley Face Girl, and Baby with a Spot on His Face. There was another baby there and his name was Trevor. He had two dads: Bald Head and Coughing Man. I wondered if there was a mix-up at the hospital about that. How come he had two dads?

Trevor ate some of the cranberry sauce. Tater did, too, and he made funny noises as he chewed, like zombie sounds.

"Do you want to eat alone in your room, Tater?" his mom said.

Tater shook his head and tried not to laugh.

"I'm not joking," she said. "Have some manners and be respectful."

All the grown-ups talked about newspaper stories and TV shows I wasn't allowed to watch and how good the stuffing was. Stuffing is food that you find inside the turkey and it looks gross, but people still eat it. Mom said my piece of turkey was too big for me. "You should only eat a piece that's as big as your hand," she said. Everyone looked at their hands.

"What about two hands?" Tater's dad asked.

"Nothing bigger than your head," Tater's mom said.

Tater's dad took a bite and closed his eyes. He called the turkey "mouthwatering," and then everyone else said, "Mouthwatering." It seemed like a weird way to describe food. Trevor couldn't say real words yet and didn't eat any turkey, but he slobbered down his chin like he was showing us what *mouthwatering* meant.

"Trevor is spitting up," Tater said. Both of the baby's dads took their napkins and wiped the slobber away.

"Do turkeys have teeth?" I asked.

"What a good question," Funny Guy said.

Smiley Face Girl said, "They don't, but they have two stomachs."

"If you put stuffing in one stomach, what is in the other?" Tater asked.

"I don't think I want to find out," Red Shirt said.

"Do turkeys eat other turkeys?" Tater asked.

"Maybe you should write a book about turkeys," Bald Head said.

"That's boring," Tater said.

After dinner there was pie. I had a piece of apple pie with whipped cream *and* ice cream. It was the best pie I've ever tasted. Tater had the same thing, so we matched, but he said he ate a whole chocolate pie once and that was his best ever. Mom wanted to go for a walk after dessert. "To walk off some of these yams," she said.

Outside, the sky looked gray in the dark, with clouds that made the stars look like small blurry dots. Tater and his mom and Maria walked with us.

"So nice to get some fresh air," Tater's mom said. Whenever someone said "fresh air," I imagined the clouds floating by, cleaning the sky like a sponge.

"Where are we going?" Tater said.

"We're going to the schoolyard and back," his mom said.

"Why?" said Tater.

"It's good to stretch your legs and take a walk after you've been cooped up all day. Walking is the best exercise."

I saw Daddy in the sky. I only saw the bottom half of his face but it was glowing, and the clouds slid by underneath like they were trying to tickle his chin. I rubbed my own chin as if the clouds were touching me. I got the feeling that even though I couldn't see his eyes, he was watching me somehow.

Tater and I pretended to be bunnies and hopped down the sidewalk. I wanted to show Daddy all the things I could do that he couldn't. I twirled around like a tornado. I kicked a rock down the sidewalk. Tater copied what I was doing, and then when he saw a grassy hill in the schoolyard, he showed me how to roll like a log. The ground was cold, but it was fun.

"Let's be turkeys," he said, but I wasn't sure how to do that, so I watched Tater crawl around in the grass for a while, making gobble sounds and moving his butt from side to side.

I looked up at Daddy to see if he was impressed. I could tell he was smiling and I could hear the *whoosh-whoosh* sounds he made sometimes. *"Whoosh whoosh whoosh!"* I said, but Tater kept making gobble sounds.

"The moon looks cool tonight," Mom said. It made me feel good when she said this, like Daddy was with us, with legs and hands and clothes and fancy hair.

"Can you kiss the moon, Mom?" I asked.

She blew a kiss to the moon. Tater acted like he was grossed out, but my heart actually became big and happy. Mom blew a hundred kisses with both hands, making smooch sounds. Tater's mom didn't kiss the moon because only my mom was allowed to do it.

"You kiss him now," Mom said to me. I jumped up and down, making kiss sounds into the sky. I wanted to ask Mom if she still loved the moon, but I was afraid she might say something sad. She hadn't talked about Daddy in a long time.

Maria whispered something to Mom that I couldn't hear and then they hugged. Tater's mom was looking down at the ground, like she wasn't supposed to see them hugging. She looked a little sad for some reason. I spun around in a circle and made a howling sound. Something somewhere howled back. Maybe some kind of animal in the schoolhouse? A couple of lights came on inside and it looked kind of spooky. I'd been inside schools before and thought they were scary. I howled some more, but no one was paying attention to me. I looked at Daddy and saw a bunch of birds flying all over his face.

"I forgot about the bats out here," said Mom.

The only bat I'd seen before was Ray, my light-up bat. I tried to remember what bats do. I knew they had some kind of superpower, like turning into vampires and zombies and breaking through glass. But there was also Batman, who fought bad guys, so maybe bats are good.

"Will they bite our necks?" Tater asked.

"Will they bite Daddy?" I asked. I didn't mean to say it out loud, but I did.

Mom looked at me and blinked her eyes a bunch, like someone trying to answer a hard question. I felt like I should say sorry, but she said, "Daddy's fine. They can't bite him. He'll be fine."

It made me think that Daddy had a shield or a force field to protect him. I had learned about force fields once and how things just bounce off them. But maybe if Daddy had a force field, it could be what kept him stuck up there, away from us.

There was more howling, and even though I could only see part of Daddy's face, I knew it was him doing it. "He's howling," I said, pointing up.

"That's the sound of their wings," Tater's mom said. "They whistle in the wind."

"Wings whistle in the wind," Tater said like a joke. But to me it still sounded like howling.

We walked back to Tater's house and said thank you for the Thanksgiving food. Tater's dad gave us some leftovers in a plastic bowl. There was cranberry sauce in there, touching everything.

29

AS FAR AS I could tell, photographs are things that stop time so you can remember stuff and either get happy or sad. There are photographs you can hold in your hand and get fingerprints on and photographs that you look at on phones or computers. For a long time, I didn't know they were the same. Mom has paper photographs of me and of us hanging on the wall and on the refrigerator, and I like to see them but I don't always remember those moments. One photo is of me on Mom's chest and there's slime all over me because I just came out of her belly button. I feel like I should remember that happening but I don't. It's funny, though, because I remember being *inside* Mom's belly, and I remember that when she ate food, it came down and plopped on my head. I don't think I'd like that very much now, but back then it felt good. Sometimes I dream about it.

Mom took pictures of a lot of things with her phone. Food, me, flowers, clothes, books, and sometimes her car in a parking lot so she wouldn't forget where she left it.

Sometimes people take photographs with old-fashioned cameras that aren't phones, and those pictures look nice, but you can't play games or call people on an old-fashioned camera. Sometimes people wear those cameras as necklaces to show people how serious they are about old-fashioned stuff. The eye part of some cameras sticks out, and sometimes they make a buzzing sound when they get sucked back in. When you push the button on an old-fashioned camera, it sends out a light that bounces back into the camera, and then God freezes time and makes a picture like a magic trick, because I guess God can do anything.

I used to think God was a man wearing a big towel, and then I thought it was an old woman, and then I thought God was a giraffe—the biggest one, with the longest neck, where everything could fit. God could make things happen anywhere.

When God makes a camera flash, sometimes it's invisible and sometimes it's so bright it hurts your eyes. If someone's eyes look like they're glowing red in a photo, it means they might be blinded. I saw a special camera once that made the photograph come out of the bottom of it and then you had to wiggle the paper in the air and count to twenty to see what you took a picture of.

Mom showed me paper pictures of her sitting on Santa Claus's lap. She was a small girl, wearing clothes that made her look like a doll. She looked like some of the little girls I saw at the park except her hair was funnier. In one photo she was smiling and reaching up to Santa's face to touch his beard. In another photo she looked scared and was squirming off his knee. "Everyone has to have a picture of themselves weeping on Santa's lap," she said.

In another photo she was a little baby looking totally calm while Santa looked like he was laughing. It could be almost any baby, but I looked in her eyes and could recognize her there. Those golden-brown spotlights were searching for something inside the camera. I don't know why, but this photo convinced me that she was exactly like me once. I looked at Mom's eyes in the picture and then at her eyes as a grown-up to see if they matched, and they did. I was glad that someone had a camera and took these pictures of Mom. "Back in the day," she said. "Back in olden times." Her hands shook when she showed me these photos. It was like her fingers were scared.

"We're going to see Santa Claus today, so you have to wear something nice," Mom said. "When you become a father someday, you can show your children your own Santa memories."

I didn't know if I was going to be a daddy someday, but maybe moms can see into the future. Or maybe only my mom since she's so smart. I wondered what would happen to me when I became a daddy. I didn't want to disappear or watch people from the sky or get killed by a monkey. I imagined myself as a normal daddy, driving a big truck, with a mustache and a ring of keys hanging from my pants. Probably some big muscles too.

At the mall with Mom, I saw dads like that with their kids. I watched how they stood, how they chewed their gum. Their hands were usually in their pockets. They were waiting in line for Santa but they had serious looks on their faces, like they were in a doctor's office waiting to get a shot. One of the things about being four years old is that I could stare at anyone for as long as I wanted. I heard it's not rude to stare unless you're over ten years old. Once you get to that age, people get mad at you for staring.

Most of the kids were with their moms, though, and those moms also looked serious, and maybe tired. Their eyes opened and closed a lot, and they looked around at everything like they were trying to remember what to get for Christmas presents.

There were two helper elves and a camera elf to take pictures. They helped Santa so he could hear every kid's wish. The camera elf was tall and had a puppet that looked like Rudolph the Red-Nosed Reindeer. If the kids were scared of Santa, he made Rudolph sing to them until they smiled. Sometimes they didn't smile, though. Sometimes they cried and he took the picture while they cried. It was true what Mom said:

everyone had to have a photograph of themselves crying on Santa's lap. I had to decide what I was going to wish for and if I was going to smile or cry. I decided on a tricycle. And I would try to smile when I asked.

"Let me see your teeth," Mom said when we got to the front of the line. I opened my mouth, and she said, "Looks good. I want to see those beautiful chompers smiling big."

I practiced for her, thinking to myself, "Do I smile with my teeth or with my lips?"

"You don't have to show all your teeth," she said. "More like this." She smiled, and I tried to count how many teeth she was showing. One of her back teeth was gold. You couldn't really see it when she smiled, but sometimes she let me see it for good luck.

"My name is Sugar Plum. What's your name?" one of the elves said to me.

"Tony Volcano," I said.

"I have a brother named Timmy Volcano," Sugar Plum said.

I was confused, but I said, "Okay."

"Get ready to say your wish, and I'll let the other elf, Holly, take you over to Santa in a moment. Do you have any questions?"

I tried to think of a good one. "Does Santa sleep here?"

"Oh, yes. Yes," she said. "Right up until Christmas Eve night."

The other elf jingled a bell and Sugar Plum walked me over to her. "Holly, this is Timmy Tornado," Sugar Plum said.

Holly, who was dressed exactly like the other elf but with curly-toed shoes, took my hand and said, "Are you ready, Timmy?"

"Tony Volcano," I said to her.

"Don't say it yet, honey. You can tell Santa what your wish

is, and if you're good, we'll give you a special candy cane after we take your picture."

She walked me over to Santa, who looked smaller than I expected. I thought his stomach would be bigger than a balloon. He smiled at me through all his white beard hair and reached out with his white-gloved hands. He picked me up and sat me on his lap.

"What's your name, little boy?" he asked me.

"I'm Tony," I said louder than usual so he'd get it right.

"Have you been a good boy this year, Tony?"

I didn't know he was going to ask me a question like that. I suddenly turned scared, wondering if I'd been "a good boy." In that moment, I understood why some kids cried. Maybe they didn't know how to answer that question. I thought about the nights I snuck out to look for Daddy when I wasn't supposed to, and I thought about hiding cookies in my room, and how I'd lost one of Tater's parachute guys in the park.

"I don't know," I said.

"Ho, ho, ho!" he said. I knew he was laughing because I could feel him jiggling. "Do you love your family and friends?" he asked.

"Yes, sir," I said.

He jiggled some more. "You can call me Santa," he said.

I looked around the big chair we were sitting in. There were large white cotton balls everywhere and Christmas presents wrapped in pretty boxes and stacked like blocks. I guessed all the cotton balls were pretend snow. Behind the chair was a big wall that looked like the inside of a house but wasn't connected to any other walls. I wondered if there was anything in the gift boxes or if they were pretend too. Maybe they were presents for the elves.

There was something that seemed fake about the whole thing, except for the Christmas tree behind Santa's chair, which

I knew was real because I could smell it. I wondered if Santa had a special toilet somewhere or if he wore a diaper.

"Do you need to go potty?" I asked him.

"Ho, ho, ho!" He said again, like he was saying the word *Oh!* backwards. "I'm doing fine, young man. I only had a little eggnog this morning."

"What's eggnog?" I asked.

"It's what happens when you drink the juice out of an egg," he said, and then raised his big white eyebrows. "Now, tell me, what do you want for Christmas?"

I looked over at Mom, who seemed both happy and worried at the same time. I looked at the other kids with their moms and dads, waiting in line for their turn.

"Um," I said. The camera elf waited for his chance to take the photograph, and I smiled at him, hoping he might do it before I let out any tears.

Tricycle, I thought in my head, but I said, "Daddy bike."

Santa looked up for a second like he was trying to figure out what I meant. Maybe he was looking for the moon, like it was there in the mall with us. I looked up too and saw a moon-shaped light bounce away from us. "Daddy bike," I said. "Big Daddy bike."

I started crying.

The camera elf pushed a button and a light blinked at us. I had cried on Santa's lap, just like Mom had cried on his lap before.

Another person who was not an elf, but had a red nose and reindeer horns, gave me a candy cane with rainbow colors and walked me and Mom behind the fake wall.

"Wait here one minute, sweetie," they said.

Mom leaned down and kissed me on the head. There was a song about Santa Claus playing on a speaker nearby, and the singer said that Santa "sees you when you're sleeping and he knows when you're awake," and it made me start crying again. I wanted to eat my candy cane but it was wrapped in plastic, so I tried to taste it through the plastic. The way it felt in my mouth made me almost throw up.

Mom laughed when the reindeer person handed her the photo. The frozen time showed me crying with my face red and my mouth wide open. Santa's mouth was open in a funny way too. It looked like we were both yawning, like we were bored of each other. It was kind of funny, but it made me sad too. What if Santa saw the picture and thought I'd gotten bored of him or was falling asleep? But another thing about the photo was that it was the first time I'd ever seen what I looked like when I cry.

Outside, on our way to the car to go home, a woman wearing a running outfit was handing out pieces of paper with someone's picture and some words written big on it. "Please call us if you see this man," she said.

Mom had a look on her face like something was wrong. "I've seen him before, at the park by the zoo," Mom told her.

"When did you see him?" the woman asked with a shaky voice.

"It's been a while," said Mom. "This summer."

I could see the picture of the man on the paper. I remembered him too. It was the old guy who gave us fruit at the park. The Chad man.

"He's been missing since yesterday," the woman said. "He missed his doctor's appointment today and we're worried about him. Please ask others if they've seen him anywhere. His family is worried."

As we walked to the car, I asked Mom, "Where did he go?"

"I don't know, but I feel bad for that woman, and for him." She looked at the paper again. "Tater's mom told me she'd met him too. And she said he was sick, so . . ."

"Maybe he's in the alley," I said. I'm not sure why I said it, but after I did, I got a bad feeling.

Later that night, after my bedtime story and after Mom went to her room and fell asleep, I got woken up by the clunky sounds of paper coming out of the fax machine. The message looked like a page from a comic book. There were squares with drawings and words in each one. I wasn't sure what the words said, and I didn't know if the fax machine knew that I couldn't read. I picked up the phone on the machine to see if anyone was there to hear me.

"Hello? Hello?" I said.

There was a purring sound, like a cat.

"I can't read the words," I said.

The purring got louder. I looked at the message closer. The drawings were a little blurry. In one square was the glowing moon. In another square was someone who looked like the Chad man. In one square was a little kid kicking a rock down a sidewalk. The next square showed the rock close up so you could see that it had a face. The other squares were too scary to look at. Pigs and garbage cans. Someone without a head, carrying a radio. One of the squares was empty. One of them was all black, like darkness.

The purring in the phone stopped. There was a ringing sound.

"Hello," I said into it. "It's me. I'm here." I didn't want to talk too loudly. "Can you hear me?" I whispered.

The ringing in the phone stopped, and a voice came on, saying, "If you'd like to make a call, please hang up and dial again." They said it twice, and then there was a clicking sound.

"What does this fax say, please?" I asked into the phone. I could hear the purring sound, and I stared at the fax, trying to figure out what it meant. I dropped the phone and pushed some of the buttons on the fax machine, hoping something else would happen.

Then I heard the voice come back on the phone and I picked it up fast.

"Don't tell your mother about this," it said. "Take this message and show it to Peter."

I didn't know whose voice it was. It sounded crunchy, like they were eating potato chips. "Who is Peter?" I asked.

The voice said the same thing again but louder and faster.

"Where is Peter?" I asked.

"Oh, Peter," the voice said. "Poor, poor Peter. Sweet, sweet Petey." And then it sounded like the voice was sad and having a hard time breathing. I waited for more information from the voice, but it just said those words again. "Oh, Peter. Poor, poor Peter. Sweet, sweet Petey."

Another fax started coming out. It was a photograph this time, but almost too dark to see what it was showing.

"What is this?" I said into the phone.

"Hold it up in the light," the voice said. "In the light of the moon."

I went to my window and tried to hold the paper so the moon could shine on it. Inside the blackness of the photograph was Dylan's face, but his eyes were closed and there was stuff coming out of his mouth. I wondered if La-La took this photo on the night she told me not to look. Why would she want to stop time on Dylan's face like this? It looked like he was sleeping and the sidewalk was under his head. I'm glad she told me not to look. I knew that even living people could be dead if they weren't careful. That's where zombies came from.

I was getting better at knowing what death is. It's like when someone is on the sidewalk and you shake them and kick them but they don't wake up.

30

MOM GOT A NEW tattoo. We were at Crown Thrift when she showed it to me. She said it was to celebrate something called the winter solstice and for the upcoming new year. It was a moon shape with two small stars next to it. "That's you and me," she said about the stars.

"And moon?" I said.

"It's a crescent moon," she said. "My favorite kind."

"I like the whole moon," I said. I touched her arm near her wrist, where the black ink still looked wet. There was some clear plastic wrapped around it so the ink could dry and become part of her skin forever.

"I like it that way too," she said. "It's funny. I used to think the whole moon looked like a glowing hole—like someone shot a hole in the sky."

"Are space people real?" I asked.

"You mean like space aliens?"

"Yes. The aliens. Like Mr. Three Eyes."

I got some alien toys for Christmas, and one of them was green and had three eyes, so I named him Mr. Three Eyes. One of the aliens had only one eye, and there was another one with no eyes but a big black helmet instead. They were fun to play with in the bathtub, which I pretended was a planet full of water.

"Aliens aren't real," Mom said. "They're made up."

"Who made them up?"

Mom tapped her chin with her finger. "Probably some scientist or a comic book guy."

When I told Tater about my Christmas presents, he said that aliens sometimes come out of guys' belly buttons. I also got a tricycle, a pizza game, and a robot that rolls on wheels until it runs into something. Tater got a computer game that he doesn't have to plug in and can play anywhere. To win the game, he had to walk through a maze to find puppies. He said it was exactly what he asked Santa Claus for.

I didn't think I would get what I asked Santa for because I messed up and said the wrong thing and cried, but somehow the tricycle was there on Christmas morning, next to the Christmas tree. I meant to stay awake that night so I could hear Santa when he came, but I must have accidentally fallen asleep. I imagined him looking in my room and trying to remember who I was and if I'd been good enough to get a tricycle. I took it outside that morning and rode it down the sidewalk right away. Mom got me a helmet and said I have to wear it when I ride, but I didn't mind because it had a lightning bolt that glows in the dark on it. And I was only allowed to ride it outside when she was with me. I wanted to keep it forever, and I dreamed about riding it to school when I was older.

I was looking at Mom's tattoo when a lady named Bernie said, "You two staying up til midnight tonight?"

Bernie was someone Mom worked with. She was new, but I liked her because she had green hair and let me eat the whipped cream off her coffee drink.

Mom made a funny sound and shrugged. "I think I'd rather sleep through it," she said. "We see time turn into the future every day anyway."

"You're so deep and wise," Bernie said.

"And tired," Mom said.

"And tired," I said, copying her.

"Did Ben tell you about The High Hat?" Bernie asked Mom.

I could see Mom's face change, like her insides were turning hard. "What about The High Hat?" she said.

"He's buying a New Year's brunch for everyone tomorrow," Bernie said.

"That's nice of him," Mom said, "but I don't think he'd want to see me there. We used to date, and it's still a little sensitive."

Bernie looked up to where Ben's office window was, but there was a curtain in the window and it was dark. "Oh, I'm sorry. I didn't know that was you."

Mom didn't say anything at first and looked up at Ben's window too. "That's why he's hardly here when I'm here," she said.

After Mom closed the store, we walked home as it was getting dark. I couldn't see Daddy in the sky anywhere. Maybe he would come out at midnight. Maybe he'd become something else for the new year. I heard people on the radio saying that they were changing for the new year somehow—like, they were going to get skinny, or get a new job as something else, or maybe stop drinking tequila. Mom said the only thing I had to do for the new year was keep growing and that would just happen automatically. I was scared of growing, though, because I didn't think my skin could stretch any more. Maybe that was why we were walking more, so my skin could get loose enough to have more muscles and places to put food.

I sort of missed being pushed in a stroller and being a baby. It had been pretty easy, actually, and the best times were when I'd be riding in the stroller, snuggled up in a blanket, looking straight up and seeing Daddy as his light followed us around.

But Mom hadn't taken me out in the neighborhood at night for a long time.

We saw people wearing fancy clothes and smiling with their mouths open. It looked like they were going to a party somewhere. They talked really loudly and said "Happy New Year!" to us. One man walked by, holding a baby like he was a dad, and said, "It's her first New Year's Eve." All this made me really curious about what happened at midnight.

"Another trip around the sun," I heard someone else say.

Does the sun come out at midnight? I wondered.

I don't really know what I thought about the sun. I once heard Dr. Duck-Duck say it burned people's eyes and skin when they weren't careful.

As we got closer to home, there were fewer people out and the sidewalk was littered with strange things: a busted lamp, spilled noodles, dirty socks, torn underwear, broken chairs, and a metal shopping cart with cans and bottles under a streetlight that buzzed and blinked off and on. Mom picked me up when I said, "Up." She kissed the top of my head. She stepped over a crutch on the sidewalk. She was walking and breathing fast.

"Do you know Peter?" I asked her.

She stopped and looked at me like she was worried about something. "Peter Johnson?" she said.

The name Peter Johnson didn't seem right. The voice on the fax machine phone didn't say the person's last name, but I knew it probably wasn't Peter Johnson. "No," I said.

"Peter Vicino?"

"No."

"Peter Hernandez?"

"No."

"Peter Ventura?"

"Yes," I said. I sensed it was the right one because it made my ears tingle.

"Who do you think he is?"

"A man," I said. "A poor man."

"Yeah," she said, and didn't say anything else.

When we got home, she made me get ready for bed. She put her pajamas on too, and said, "It's going to turn into a new year while we sleep tonight. When we wake up, we can do our own countdown."

She started telling me a bedtime story. Sometimes she read out of a book, but I liked it more when she told me one without reading it off paper. On this night she told me a story of a little boy who wakes up at night, floats naked into a kitchen, and then almost gets turned into a cake. At the end of it she said, "And they lived happily ever after," but I was never sure what that meant. When she finished telling me the story, she drew a tattoo on my arm: a crescent moon and two stars.

That night, loud music woke me up. It was coming from an apartment close to ours. I wanted to get up and see what was happening. Maybe it was midnight and the sun had come out. Maybe I grew in my sleep and someone was celebrating. Then I heard the sound of a gun being shot outside or firecrackers. Loud bangs and people cheering. I stayed in bed and covered my whole body with my blanket and tried to remember how to do a countdown. It was like counting, but backwards.

When I woke up in the morning, I went to wake up Mom, but she was already up. There was a small cup of my favorite grape juice on the table and she was pouring coffee into a cup for herself. She looked at me and took a sip from her cup. Then she took a deep breath and said, "Peter Ventura is your dad's name."

31

PETER VENTURA was the name I listened for. I was almost afraid to say it out loud, as if someone would hear me say it and tell me something bad. I didn't even say it to Tater when he came over with his mom, like I was keeping a secret from him. Instead we talked about magic. He said he saw a magician at the zoo, and it was kind of scary. But he couldn't stop talking about him. Tater said he made a tiger disappear and then made an elephant levitate. I wondered if the tiger became a ghost. But mostly I felt bad for the elephant.

Tater had a deck of cards he got for Christmas, and he was trying to show me a magic trick with them. "Pick a card," he said. "Any card."

I picked one that had a red heart and a number three on it. He told me to show him the card and then put it back in the cards. I showed him the card and heard him whisper to himself, "Three hearts." After I put it back in the deck, he said, "Abra Camera!" and waved his arms around in the air. Then he looked through all the cards until he found the card I'd picked. The number three, red hearts.

"Is this the card you picked?" he asked.

"Yes. Wow," I said.

"Mom!" Tater yelled out to the other room. "I did a magic!"

"Proud of you, T!" his mom yelled back.

"Let's call someone," Tater said to me, looking at the fax machine. He picked up the phone part and pushed some buttons. There were some beeping sounds that didn't sound good. "This is a cool toy because it looks like it's from the future far, far away," he said.

"It's not a toy," I said, wanting him to stop touching it. "It's a fax machine."

"I know that," Tater said. "It's for mature kids."

Mom came in my room and said, "What do you guys want for dinner? Tater's going to spend the night."

Tater got up and did a funny dance. He made up a song: "I'm gonna spend the ni-ight. I'm gonna spend the ni-ight!"

After we ate dinner—pizza with extra cheese—we picked a movie to watch. It was a cartoon about a boy who lived in the jungle and didn't have parents but was friends with a panther, a wolf family, and a singing bear. The bad guys were the tiger and the snake. There were no pigs or rats in the jungle. At the end the boy leaves the jungle and sees a girl for the first time. He walks away from his jungle friends and goes with the girl so he can get regular human clothes and maybe get married and become a daddy.

When it was time to go to sleep, Tater kept making me laugh by saying funny things like "Mean cheeeeeese" and then farting in his sleeping bag. "Don't worry," he said. "It doesn't smell." When we stopped cracking up, it got quiet for a minute and then we burst out laughing again for no reason. Mom let me sleep in a sleeping bag on the floor too. Maybe that's why I was laughing so much.

Tater said it was like we were camping in the jungle. "Pretend the walls are trees," he said. Mom had already told us to be quiet once, but it was hard to stop talking and laughing. It was like we were in a contest to see who could stay awake the longest. Then it was silent for a while and Tater farted without laughing, so I knew he must finally be asleep for real.

I wanted to go outside and look for Daddy, so I quietly put on my clothes and even my furry hat and gloves in case it was cold. I watched Tater for a whole minute to make sure he was asleep. It was funny to look at him when he was sleeping. He slept sideways, and I noticed his hair was getting pretty long. He looked like the Mowgli kid in the jungle movie. I looked at his ear closely and thought it was shaped wrong. I touched my own ear to see if it was the same way. Mine was rounder. Even though he was a year older than me, we were about the same size. Mom had actually told me that day that I'd had a growth spurt and was going to have to get new clothes again.

Before I left I decided to grab Ray in case I needed his light. I squeezed him to make sure he still worked. I opened my door without making a sound, but Tater suddenly woke up.

"Tony, what are you doing?"

I didn't know how to explain myself. I said I was going to the bathroom, even though I was wearing my shoes and furry hat.

"What are you doing with your bat?" he asked.

"He's my light," I said.

"Oh," said Tater.

We were both silent, squinting at each other. I hoped he would fall back asleep so I could sneak out.

"I want to go too," he said.

We walked on our tiptoes to the bathroom with Ray giving us light to see in the dark. We knew not to wake up Mom.

"You go first," I said. The potty seat was down, but Tater looked into the toilet like he was looking for something in the water.

"I don't have to," he said. He stepped back so I could use the toilet, even though I didn't really have to go either. I stood on the little step in front of the toilet and unzipped my pants. Tater was standing behind me, waiting.

"I have to sit down," I said.

"I'll wait right here," Tater said, turning away a little. His voice sounded a little nervous for some reason.

I sat on the potty seat and pretended to be pooping. I grunted a little bit and watched Tater to make sure he didn't turn around.

"Are you doing it?" he asked.

"Almost done," I said. I breathed hard like I was blowing out candles and made more sounds.

"Can I hold your bat?" Tater asked.

"Just a second, please," I said. I got off the toilet and zipped my pants up. "Here," I said, handing him Ray. He squeezed Ray's belly and the light from the bat body glowed on his face.

"Can I see your poop?" Tater said. He looked at the toilet and I got worried because there was no poop to see.

"I already flushed," I said.

Tater kept looking at the toilet. My special potty seat was blue and plastic. I was the only one who used it because Mom took it off to use the grown-up seat when she had to go. She never peed standing up.

"I didn't hear you flush," Tater said.

"I did," I said. "It's a silent flusher."

We tiptoed back to my room and then Tater said, "Do you have any cookies?"

"I don't know where they are," I said. Tater seemed pretty awake. This was only the third time he had spent the night. I looked at my window. There were curtains with yellow flowers on them, but they weren't closed all the way. I thought I saw Daddy out there.

"Do you want to go outside?" I asked Tater.

32

TATER HAD NEVER seen anyone sleep on a sidewalk at night before. There were a couple of people under blankets outside closed-down stores and offices. Some of them had shopping carts and road cones holding up giant plastic sheets, and others had really big tents. Orange and yellow and all sorts of colors, all the way down the street. Some had pets inside their tents—mean-looking dogs, cats on leashes, and lizards. Some of the sidewalk people were still awake, sitting on lawn chairs and drinking or eating together—doughnuts, potato chips, and sandwiches. There was an opened box of pizza outside of one tent and it looked like someone had spilled beer all over it. One of the big tents was lit up from inside, as if someone was burning a candle. Some of the sidewalk people looked at me like they recognized me, but they usually left me alone. Maybe they thought Dylan was my brother and I lived with him in the alley. Usually if someone was sleeping in the alley, they were probably extra sick. People coughed and moaned more when they were in the alley, and it smelled pretty bad in there, mostly from the garbage cans and throw-up.

"Do you ever get scared out here?" Tater asked.

"Sometimes," I said. "But I'm used to it."

Before we snuck out, I talked Tater into coming with me because I knew he wouldn't want to be left alone without me

and that would have meant I couldn't go. I told him I go outside at night all the time and that my mom lets me but that we
still shouldn't wake her up. I told him the sidewalk people
aren't scary and sometimes they even show you toys you've
never seen before. I told him that when the moon was full you
could see a face on it and pretend it was anyone in the world,
up in the sky like a superhero. I didn't tell him about the moon
being my dad and that sometimes he talked to me.

"Do you know these people?" Tater asked.

"Yeah," I said, though I mostly didn't. I just wanted to get
down the street, where I would see Daddy better.

"What's his name?" Tater asked, pointing to a man making
a sign out of a big piece of cardboard. The man looked up and
waved.

I didn't know the man's name but I said, "That's Bob," and
tried to walk faster.

"Hi, Bob!" Tater called out.

"Hey, big boy," the man called back. "Can you help me
with this?"

"Keep walking," I said. Tater waved really fast and kept
going with me.

"How do you spell *surgery*?" the man yelled in our direction.

A rat peeked its head out of a sack on the sidewalk, and I
could tell Tater was afraid, which made me act braver. We
crossed the street and walked by some beat-up suitcases, an
old TV, people in sleeping bags zipped all the way up, and a
bike missing its front wheel, tied loosely with a rope to a pole.
We were getting close to the parking lot where I could get a
good view of Daddy. I looked up to make sure he was still
there. I didn't know if he would say anything to Tater or if he
would only talk to me.

"Are there more people than houses in our city?" Tater
asked. It was funny when he asked me questions since he was

older and probably smarter, but because I had seen the outside world at night, maybe I was smarter about some things. What I saw in the neighborhood during the day and what it looked like at night were very different from each other. Tater probably hadn't seen this kind of nighttime world, so it was like he only knew half the real story.

"I think there are a lot of houses and a lot of people, but they don't know each other," I said, but I wasn't sure what I was trying to mean.

Tater looked down at the sidewalk as we walked, like he was trying to find something.

"I guess," he said, "if you have a lot of money, you could buy a house or apartment. So the president should just make more money for everyone."

I hadn't thought of that before. But maybe there weren't enough machines to make money with or people to turn the machines on.

"Or," he said, "they could have sleepovers with people that have houses. Then they could be happier and have a better place to put their stuff. And they could go to the bathroom and take baths and have friends."

In the big parking lot, I concentrated on Daddy. His light was bright but kind of blinking, like he was tired and might fall asleep or disappear. I wondered if we had to worry about pigs being out.

"What's your dad's name?" I asked Tater.

"His name is Shawn, remember?" Tater said. "I told you before. My mom's name is Sean, too, but her name isn't spelled right. Says my dad, anyway."

"My dad's name is Peter," I said.

"Where is he at?" Tater asked.

I tried to think of the right way to say it.

"You don't have to tell me," Tater said. His voice sounded

like he'd done something wrong, like it wanted to go back in his mouth.

"He's close," I said. "I think. Look up. Maybe he's there." I pointed at the moon.

"I hope he is there too," Tater said. "Wouldn't it be cool if he was an astronaut and we could see him flying around up there?"

A dog started barking loudly at us from somewhere close. Tater and I screamed like we'd been zapped by lightning. The barking was coming from a big dog that was sticking its head out of an old car in the middle of the parking lot. The car didn't have a windshield or a hood and one of the back doors was open. The dog jumped out of the car and barked more as it walked toward us. There wasn't anywhere for us to hide, so I held Ray up and made his light come on. I hoped the dog was scared of bats.

"Tony," Tater said. "Do you know whose dog this is?"

I didn't, but for some reason it looked familiar. It stopped barking and walked toward us slowly. It wagged its tail. It looked much taller than us, as big as a cow. Brown hair on its back and soft-looking white hair in front and on its chest. Brown legs with heavy fluffed-up paws. It looked like it could walk over us without jumping. It wore an old leather collar with a metal tag attached to it. I pretended like I knew who the dog was.

"His name is Dylan," I said.

"Good boy, Dylan," Tater said. "You're a good boy."

Inside my jacket were some of my favorite snacks: pretzel nuggets with peanut butter inside them. I threw a couple of them so the dog had to turn to fetch them. Then Tater and I quickly tried to run away. If we could get back to the sidewalk people, maybe they would protect us if the dog tried to eat us. But the dog caught up and stayed close behind us, not even running really—just following like he wanted to hang out with us.

"Wait for me," a voice said.

I looked back and the dog looked right at me.

"Did you say that?" I said.

The dog stopped and sat politely. He looked at us, his tongue sticking out, slobbering and funny.

"Dylan, are you a guard dog?" Tater asked. He sounded nervous. I heard the sound of those words: *guard dog*. It sounded like "god dog." I wondered if dogs had their own god.

The dog lifted his paw in the air, like he wanted to shake hands. I held his paw and he let me move it up and down. He stood up on his hind legs for a second and looked around like he didn't want anyone to see us. Then the dog looked at Tater and lifted his paw for him. Tater grabbed the paw but held it nervously, as if it might scratch him. The dog rested his big head on top of Tater's head and sniffed the air. Tater was shaking and crying. The dog rubbed his face gently on Tater's face to dry the tears.

I heard a *whoosh-whoosh* sound and a bell ringing lightly somewhere. I looked at the moon and saw its bright light coming down. There were shadows on the concrete that looked like holes in the ground, and they were growing bigger. The dog looked at the moon too. He was smiling kind of like a human, like he'd start laughing if you told him a good joke. I climbed on top of the dog and held on to his collar like I wanted to ride him. Like a cowboy on a horse. Tater got on too, and held on to my shoulders from behind. The dog rose up and walked, his four legs moving easily and carefully so we didn't fall off. It seemed like we were up very high—high enough to get hurt if we fell off. The dog stayed in the light and dodged the shadows on the ground. He carried us into the middle of the empty street. We moved past all the sidewalk people, back in the direction of home. They were all awake now, standing next to their tents and brightly colored plastic sheets. They watched us from both sides of the street, and the spotlight of the moon made us look magical. None of them spoke or looked away. A couple of cockroaches appeared on the street, and the dog crushed them with his giant paws. I wondered if this was how a king felt.

The light of the moon was slowly disappearing, and I looked up to see the face on the moon close its eyes.

"Daddy, talk," I said.

"Mister Peter?" Tater said.

The sky turned dark then, and the dog quickly sat. Tater let go of me and slid down the dog's back like it was a slide. I let go of the dog's collar and slid off too. The dog lifted his chin and howled at the dark sky like he was trying to call the light back. All the sidewalk people got back into their tents or under their plastic roofs. Tater and I were alone on the street now, and we watched the shape of the dog run away from us, back in the direction of the parking lot.

It was so quiet as we walked home, the sound of nothing almost sounded like something. One time at Crown Thrift, Mom showed me a seashell for the first time. I had to hold it with both hands when she told me to put the open part of it against my ear. She said that's what the ocean sounds like, and I couldn't remember what the ocean even was, so the sound made me scared because I thought it was the sound of a monster that breathes weird.

That's what this night sounded like, walking home in the dark with Tater. Silence turned up. When Tater said, "We better hold hands so we don't lose each other," his words cut into the air like a siren. His hand was wet and his fingers cold.

We snuck back into the apartment and walked softly back to my room. When we were back in our sleeping bags, Tater said, "Is Dylan really a dog?" but I didn't say anything back. I pretended I was already asleep, until I really fell asleep.

In the morning, we didn't talk about what happened. I kept thinking he was going to say something to Mom as she made us scrambled eggs for breakfast, but he didn't. After we ate, we watched the jungle movie again as we waited for Tater's mom to pick him up. I liked watching movies more than one time. It was like practicing for something and getting better at it. It made me feel smarter, like I knew so much about the world. Like I was a kid who tricked animals and walked out of the jungle by myself.

33

I DIDN'T LIKE taking naps anymore, but sometimes Mom made me. When I started going to preschool, which was fun, I had to take naps there too. At least when I took naps at home, sometimes Mom would nap with me, or at least she'd pet my head, which was probably my favorite feeling in the world. I hoped she would still pet my head when I grew up and still take naps with me. Maybe I could pet her head, too, when my hands got bigger.

Sometimes, when I was only a little bit asleep at nap time I'd listen to what she was watching on TV or I'd hear her talking on the phone. Sometimes she talked to herself or sat at the kitchen table, writing or drawing. I could actually hear her drawing sometimes—all the pencils she used, scratching or tapping in her notebook.

One time I was sneaky, and I saw one of her drawings when she went to the bathroom. It was a face that looked like hers but the eyes were colored blue instead of brown and her lips were a brighter red than her own. The way she drew the hair was different, too—more wavy and fancy-looking, like someone on TV. It looked like it was blowing in the wind or maybe she was flying. It was only a picture of the face, so it was hard to tell what the rest of the body was doing. I looked at it until I heard the bathroom door open, and then I got back on the floor and pretended to play with my Legos again.

Mom said when I turn five years old I can probably stop taking naps. But, she said, in the meantime naps would help me grow up.

We were on her bed, and she was reading a book to me about an outer-space alien who was lost on the wrong planet, and I closed my eyes and thought about myself on a different planet. This other planet was full of eggs that rolled around looking for salt. When they found the salt, they rolled through it and their shell changed to gold. When they became gold, part of their shell opened up and human legs came out so they could dance and be happy. The planet was full of sad white rolling eggs and happy golden dancing eggs. Because I was the only human, I had to take some of the broken egg parts off the ground and make them into a fake egg suit. If the real eggs found out I was human, they would turn me into salt.

Then I heard Mom's voice in another room and realized I'd been dreaming.

"It's hard to have an answer when you never know what the future will show us," she said.

Another voice said, "Anyone can say that. What you just said is true for all people, all the time. That's why you have to have faith."

"I do have faith," Mom said. "That's why I don't want to give an answer I'll be stuck in. I know that drives you crazy, and I'm sorry, Ben."

She was talking to Ben in the front room. For some reason, I felt happy about this. I wanted to get up and go out there. I missed Ben, which surprised me. I hadn't seen him in a long time and I wanted to see what he looked like. Was he taller? Did he get fat? Was his hair green? Did he still crouch over like he was wearing a really heavy backpack?

"I'm going to go away, too, then," Ben said. "It'll be easier for me if I don't live so close to you. I'm thinking of Minnesota."

"Minnesota? Why there?"

"I've always wanted to go there. I'm ready to live somewhere cold. There has to be . . . I don't know."

"You don't know what?"

"There has to be more distance separating us," he said. "Mountains and miles. Rivers. Time zones. I don't know."

I could tell they were getting impatient with each other. Whenever people say "I don't know" a bunch of times, it means something isn't perfect. But I got the feeling that even when something's perfect, it makes for other problems. Maybe Mom didn't really want to have a boyfriend right then. It reminded me of a song I heard that said, "Life is a mystery. Everyone must stand alone."

"I don't know what else to do," Ben said. "I have to protect my heart, and that's hard to do when I live nine blocks away from you *and* work with you!"

"I understand," Mom said. "Please don't be loud. Tony's taking a nap." There was something in her voice that sounded broken.

"I should have known it wasn't going to work when we started seeing each other," Ben said. "I could tell you were still waiting for him. And then when you sent the ring back to me, it really hurt."

Mom didn't say anything.

"It really hurt," Ben said again.

I couldn't think of what ring he was talking about, and then I realized it must have been what was inside the box he gave her on her birthday, with all the crumpled-up paper. I remembered the time at the mall when Ben asked the person at the diamond store about the rings that cost a lot of money, and I wondered if he got it there. At the time I didn't like Ben, but maybe he was okay after all. It was easy to see why guys would want to fall in love with Mom. She was the prettiest girl I'd seen, except for Tammy Bridgewater, the girl who talked about the weather on TV. Even Tater liked her.

I could hear Ben making sad sounds out there. Mom was talking quietly to him, but I couldn't hear what she said. Then she turned the radio on low and I heard the door of her room close. I got up and slowly peeked out to see if Ben was still out there, but he wasn't. Instead, I heard their muffled voices coming from Mom's room. I went to the kitchen and grabbed a juice box from the fridge. The control thing for the TV was hidden somewhere, but I sat on the couch and acted like I was watching a show anyway. I saw my face on the dark screen, so I pretended it was a show about me. In the show, I was a cat with a boy's head and I climbed all over everything.

I made purring sounds that kept getting louder, until I realized they weren't coming from me. It sounded like they were coming from Mom's room. I walked over and put my ear on the door because you can hear through the wood better that way. But my head accidentally hit the door, and it sounded like a knock. I ran back and jumped on the couch as Mom opened her door. She looked at me and then looked around nervously like there might be someone else in the apartment. "Did you knock on the door, honey?" she asked me.

I didn't know what to say except no.

"Hmm," she said, and looked around again. "What are you doing?"

"Watching TV."

Mom looked at the TV, which wasn't turned on. "Good show?" she said.

I looked at her and tried to figure out if Ben was going to come out of her room or if he was hiding.

"It's about a cat," I said. "With a boy's head. He's taking a nap."

"Sounds fun," she said

"Yeah," I said. "It's pretty good." I could hear noises from her room—something rustling around, a small cough. Mom coughed, too, and then closed her door like she was trying to cover up the sounds.

"I'm going to get a bath ready for you," she said.

"I don't want one," I said. What I wanted was to know what was going on. Why wouldn't she let Ben out?

"I got bubbles," she said. She could tell I was being cranky. I do love bubble baths.

She walked over and tickled me until I was squirming around and almost laughing. It made me almost pee my pants and I thought I'd better go to the bathroom before I actually did. I wanted to hold it in but didn't think I could. I ran to the bathroom and shouted, "Be right back!"

"Get your clothes off and get ready for a bubble party!" Mom shouted back. I heard her bedroom door squeak open and then the front door open and close before I was done peeing. When I came back out, Mom's bedroom door was open again and her room looked messy, but no one was in there. I looked at Mom with squinted eyes, like I was trying to figure out her trick. I wanted to ask her if someone was in her room, but she had a look on her face like she was tired and impatient and might get mad.

Mom went in the bathroom and turned on the water for my bath. She grabbed a plastic bottle that looked like a penguin and squirted stuff out of it that turned into bubbles. The water turned into a fluffy cloud. I got naked and waited as it grew bigger and bubblier. Mom turned off the water and checked it with her hand to make sure it wasn't too hot. Before I got in, I asked, "Where is Ben?"

"He isn't here," she said.

"But where is he?"

"Minnesota."

"What's Minnesota?" I asked.

"It's a cold place with Vikings and Timberwolves," she said.

"Is he going to be okay?"

"He'll be fine."

I stood there naked. Mom did her smile that looked more sad than happy.

"Where is Daddy?" I asked.

"He's out there, in the sky," she said, like it was an easy answer. "We'll go see him soon."

It had been a long time since she said we'd see him. It seemed different, though, the way she said it this time. More like real life and not just imagination and wishes. Her eyes looked different too. They grew bigger when she said "soon." They looked like moons. They looked like planets or stars. My heart was beating faster.

"What's his name?" I asked. I already knew the answer but I wanted to hear her say it again.

"Peter Ventura."

She picked me up and put me in the bubbles. She dipped her hand in them and put a bunch on my head, like a hat.

"Do you think Peter Ventura is like us?" I asked her.

"I don't know," she said. "I think so. You'll have to ask him yourself."

34

ONE MORNING, the fax machine was gone. I woke up and didn't see it anywhere. I asked Mom if she knew where it was, and she said she hadn't seen it.

"It was in my room," I said, "the thing I played telephone with."

She looked at me blankly. I felt like I was missing something I needed, like I'd lost a friend trying to help me. Someone who gave me clues.

"I didn't do anything with your fax machine," Mom said.

I thought she was lying to me but I wasn't sure why. Maybe she saw a message that told her to throw it away. "Did you leave it somewhere?" she asked.

I couldn't believe how she was acting. I was breathing extra fast, and she told me to calm down and count to ten. I kept saying, "Mom, you know. Mom, you know."

She said we could go out and look for it, and I said okay because I thought we should look in all the garbage cans and in the alley too.

Our neighborhood looked different that day. There weren't any tents or sleeping bags. A lot of the places that looked old and empty at night had nice clean windows and people working in them. There was a coffee shop, a place full of fancy paper and birthday cards, a shoe store, a store that sold beds and pillows, a sandwich shop, an antique store, a place for people to drink wine, another coffee shop that also sold ice cream, a clothing store, and a bookstore.

We went into the antique store and Mom asked the woman working if they had any fax machines. The woman said they didn't because they weren't antiques yet. There were a couple of garbage cans on the streets, but they were nearly empty. No fax machines or even fax paper.

The air was cool but the sky was blue and sunny as we walked down the street. There were newly painted benches everywhere, with strong-looking trees next to them and flower-pots with flowers blooming in them. A person wearing all-white clothes waved at us from one corner, eager to give us coupons for a new grocery store. We walked by the alley, and I hardly recognized it. There was no garbage on the ground, no throw-up or empty bottles or people sleeping next to shopping carts. No rats or pigs. No fax machine.

I felt suspicious, like something wasn't right. The way everything looked clean and happy made me dizzy. I looked all over, hoping to see something dirty or messy.

Mom didn't say anything. She watched me look around as I became more confused. She put her hand gently on my head and said, "I can get you a play phone. It'll be better than a fax machine."

"It wasn't just a phone," I said.

Mom shrugged and squeezed my shoulder.

We walked a couple of blocks more, and then Mom said she wanted to get something to eat, so we went into a Mexican restaurant. It looked a lot like Banjo's but it seemed bigger and nicer inside, and there was a man in one corner playing a guitar. Mom said we could share a breakfast burrito and I could have a horchata. The woman who took our order looked like Angela, the woman who worked at Banjo's, but I wasn't sure. She looked right in my eyes while Mom paid. If it was Angela, I thought she'd recognize me, but she didn't say anything. Maybe I looked different than I did before. She looked different for sure. Her clothes looked brand-new and her face was more cheerful. I wasn't sure if this was Banjo's, but I liked it better the way it was before.

"When you had the fax machine, what did it do?" Mom said when we sat down.

"It made a map to where Daddy is."

"Really?"

"Yeah, and it made me a sign, so people could help me," I said. "And it made weird sounds and talked to me through the phone part."

"Help you in what way?"

"To find Daddy."

She had a look on her face like she was thinking of another question. The man with the guitar walked over to us and started playing a song. He sang, "Here comes the sun. Doo doo doo doo. Here comes the sun. La la la la." Mom gave him a dollar and a funny look, and he went back to the corner.

Our breakfast burrito was delivered to us at the table and it was so good that Mom ordered another one.

On the walk home the sun shined directly in our path. I noticed, for the first time, the sidewalk sparkling with dots of silver, like twinkling stars. We were both wearing sunglasses and people waved to us and said hello. A police officer eating a muffin smiled and gave us a salute. I heard wind chimes, birds, and laughter. The breeze that drifted through our hair smelled like fresh-baked cookies.

As we got closer to home, Mom pulled out her phone and saw it buzzing with Maria's name on it. She answered it, and I could hear Maria's voice talking for a long time. When Mom got off the phone, she looked at me with a strange face. It looked like she was going to be sick.

"Maria's coming over," she said.

"Is she okay?" I asked.

"Something's wrong," she said. "But she couldn't tell me."

"But she's going to tell you when she comes over?"

"Yes," she said. Then she looked down at me and smiled with her mouth but not her eyes. "It'll be okay, Tony. You can watch a show when she gets here."

When we got home, Mom turned her computer on and searched for something. She was blocking the screen with her back to me so I couldn't see what she was looking at. She typed fast and her shoulders were hunched up tight like she was sucking her breath in but not breathing out. She looked at her phone and typed something on there too. I was on the floor, looking through a book of cute pictures of animals sleeping. If I showed Mom one of the pictures, maybe she'd feel better.

"Mom, look at this tired bear," I said.

She didn't look right away, and when she did, she didn't smile.

"I'm sorry, Tony. I'll have to look at that book with you later. I have to focus on something else right now."

Not being able to make Mom feel better gave me a nervous feeling, like I'd done something wrong. It made me wonder how long it would be before she smiled again.

Maria also looked and acted different than usual when she came over. Her face looked gray and sleepy, and she did that thing with her mouth that grown-ups do when they try to hide how they feel. Her best friend, Carmen, was with her. I liked Carmen because she once let me make a painting with her using real paints and brushes. Maria told me Carmen was going to take me to the park for a little bit, so I put my jacket and sunglasses back on and we walked to the park.

"Why do you have to take me to the park?" I asked Carmen.

"Your mom will tell you about it later," she said.

"But do you know why?" I asked.

"I can't say," she said. "But your mom or Aunt Maria will tell you later. Let's have fun at the park while the sun's still bright."

It was the same park I always went to, the one I played at with Tater sometimes. I was getting kind of bored of it. I wished it had a bigger slide and a merry-go-round that wasn't lopsided. I wished we could go to a different park.

Carmen pushed me on the swing. She hummed a happy-sounding song as she did. There was no one else at the park. "Want me to do an underdog?" she asked.

An underdog is when the person pushing you on the swing gives you a push so high they can run underneath you. It's the best thing about getting pushed on a swing if you're not scared to do it. I've always loved underdogs, even when I was in the baby swings. But I said, "No, I don't want an underdog."

She stopped humming and we didn't say anything for a while. Then she asked me, "What's your favorite thing about the park?"

"The man who gave us fruit," I said.

"I think I heard about that man," she said.

"He got sick," I said.

"Oh?"

"Yeah. The Chad man. He's not alive anymore."

I didn't know which way described it better. Do you say, "He's dead," or "He's not alive"? It sounds like different things. I think people who are alive can feel dead, but I don't think people who are dead can feel alive.

I still saw posters on telephone poles with Chad's face on

it, though. They said that he was missing, so maybe he wasn't dead. He was somewhere between dead and alive, I guessed. I was always glad to see his picture on the posters, even if they were worn out and hard to read. People still hoped they might see him someday.

35

MARIA SAID SHE wanted to explain something to me because Mom couldn't right then. Mom stayed in her room, away from everyone. She needed time and space to think and to grieve.

"Do you know what 'grieve' means?" Maria asked.

I thought about it and said, "Is it when you're mad or sad about something?"

"That's exactly right," Maria said. "Adults have to do it, and kids sometimes have to grieve things too."

"Yeah, I get grieved at things a lot," I said.

"Well, grieving usually means when you're really super sad because sometimes really bad things happen."

"Did something really bad happen?" I asked.

"I have to tell you about your father," she said.

"Was his name Peter Ventura?"

Maria looked over at Mom's bedroom door. It was closed but we could still hear Mom making crying sounds.

"Sometimes good people get in trouble for something bad people have done," she said. "You know what I mean?"

I remembered a time I got in trouble because this kid at a birthday party lost a Hot Wheels car and said I took it from him. And then other people thought I'd taken it and that I was lying about it, but the next day the kid found it in his brother's coat pocket and the kid had to say he was sorry to me on speakerphone. I didn't want to tell Maria that whole story though, so I just nodded.

Maria reached over and touched my cheek like she wanted to make sure I was paying attention.

"Your dad, when your mom met him, was a good man," she said. "But he wasn't perfect, and he hung around some people who weren't good people."

"Bad people?" I said.

"Maybe not *bad* people," she said, "but people who do bad things. Not smart. I mean, it's okay to make mistakes, but sometimes people make mistakes because they're not thinking, and then they feel weird about those mistakes and they start making mistakes on purpose because the first mistake embarrasses them. Also because they can't help it. Sometimes people don't know better."

I watched Maria's eyes as she talked. It looked like she was sad, and I thought I could see tears, but they stayed there inside her eyes somehow.

"There was a guy named Landry, a friend of your dad's, and he was a guy whose job it was to look for people and, um, talk to them. Like, to solve problems. Kind of like a cop. I mean, he used to be a policeman, this Landry guy. But this was different."

"Is my dad a policeman?" I asked.

"He wanted to be," Maria said. "He almost was, but you have to train really hard and take a bunch of tests to become one, and he was almost done doing all that, but then he broke a rule and got in trouble. So, no, he wasn't a policeman. But he worked with Landry and they would, you know, solve problems for people."

"Like math problems?"

"Yeah, sure, like math problems." Maria smiled for a second, but at the same time a tear fell out of her eye and she wiped it away quick. "One day, they went to a man's house to talk to him, and this man—his name was Red—had been lying to folks and owed a lot of money to people. But Red kept saying he wouldn't pay, and Landry got angry. Your dad tried to calm things down, but Red ran into another room of his house and brought out a gun. It got really reckless, and Red shot at Landry and your dad, but he didn't hit them. Then Landry got to him and took the gun away. He gave the gun to your dad and then started, uh . . . fighting Red. You know, with his hands."

"Did Daddy shoot the gun?" I asked.

"Well, no. He knew he didn't have to shoot. He only held it up, to keep Red from attacking them again. But Landry was really mad, and he did something you should never do to anyone or anything."

"What did he do?"

Maria looked like she was trying to figure out what to say next. It was quiet for a while, and we heard Mom crying louder through the walls.

"He started a fire," Maria said. "He started a fire on the man. Red got burned. Your dad broke it up though. Pushed Landry away, put out the fire, and basically saved Red's life. In fact, Landry tried starting a fight with your dad then too. Your dad got the better of him though, and then got out of there."

"Did Daddy have to go to the hospital?"

"No, but the police came looking for him the next day. And that's when the story got really weird. Red told the police that Pete—your dad—set the fire and tried to kill him. Landry, or maybe someone else, must have threatened him so he'd change his story. Your dad still had burn marks on his shirt and his fingerprints were on the gun, and now both of those guys invented some story so Pete would get sent to jail. It was right before you were born, and he wanted to be a good father."

"So is my dad in jail?" I asked.

Maria rubbed her eyes and they made a squishy wet sound. She put her hands over her whole face like she was trying to shape it into something else. Then she breathed in and out really hard.

"He did go to jail," she said. "It was a mistake. Sometimes things really don't go the way they should. Grown-ups can lie in this world, Tony, and it makes things unfair. When people find themselves in trouble, they have to go to a court and people tell their part of the story, and then a judge decides who gets punished and for how long. Both Red and Landry said it was your dad who shot the gun and set Red on fire. Red's face was pretty bad, like melted and weird. He could barely talk."

"Do faces melt off all the way?" I asked.

"Not really, honey. But it's terrible when someone's face gets hurt for life like that."

"Does my daddy have a face?"

"Your daddy got sentenced to ten years in prison because those men lied. But some of the truth was found out recently and they were going to let him out. He was going to come home and be with you again—with your mom and you."

I wanted to know the end of the story. I wanted to know it right then. My stomach was tumbling. Maria wouldn't look at me, and I saw her hands shaking.

"Does my daddy have a face?" I asked again.

"Your father was attacked in prison yesterday," she said. "They burned him."

I wanted to lie down on the carpet. I wanted to yell as loud as I could into the ground. I wanted to be with Mom so she could hold me. I wanted to see if the moon was out. I wanted to see if it looked different. If it was still alive.

"Your father is still alive," Maria said. "He wants to stay alive. He's in the hospital, in a burn unit. He's in surgery, probably for today and tomorrow both. They're working on his face, and his chest and back."

She took me by the shoulders and pulled me to her chest. I was wobbly, but she held tight and we both cried.

"We have to be strong and brave right now, especially for your mom. Think healing thoughts and be positive if you can. He loves you very much and he wants to come home. He wants to see you."

"I want to be with Mom," I said. "Can we please see Mom?"

"Let me see how she's doing," Maria said. She knocked on Mom's bedroom door, and it opened a little. Mom and Maria talked quietly to each other and I heard Maria say, "I told him, and now he wants to see you."

Mom opened the door more and said, "Come here, Tony." She picked me up and put me on her bed. Maria came in too. "Stay," Mom said to her.

The three of us lay on the bed, letting our tears come out. Mom was holding my hand, and her hand was cold. I listened to the sounds of all of us breathing—heavy and shaky and scared. I thought of Daddy breathing and hoped it sounded the same.

I tried to imagine I was weightless, like an angel. I fell asleep.

Outside, the day turned to night. The sky was clear and full of stars that got brighter as the darkness grew. Mom was at her bedroom window, looking out. She grabbed my coat and lifted me off the bed. Maria was still sleeping, curled up like a circle. We went outside, and Mom said, "Hop on my back."

I held on tight as we went down the street, to the old parking lot, where we could see the moon. I wondered if the moon was ever really Daddy. I remembered the moon talking to me. I remembered the nights when there was no moon. And the one night when there were three different moons.

"We're here," Mom said. She sat down and then lay back on the concrete, on top of a faded white line. She put her arms behind her head and stared into the sky. "You can use me as a pillow," she said, patting her stomach. I rested my head there, and I could feel her ribs. For some reason, this gave me a memory of breastfeeding and the taste of her milk.

I studied the soft-glowing moon and tried to imagine what Daddy would look like. The face seemed to be moving around and blurring, like it was trying to tell us something.

"What is the moon saying?" I asked.

"We have to find Polaris," Mom said.

"Who's that?" I asked.

"It's the North Star. It's a good one to wish on."

"Where is it?"

She pointed, but I wasn't sure which one it was. There were so many dots of light.

"Now wish," she said.

The moon became brighter and made it hard to see anything. Its light took over the sky and made it almost seem like day. The face of the moon was all white, without a face. No mouth to talk. A spotlight beaming. I turned my head away. Mom's belly was a pillow I pressed into. She put her hand on my head and petted me.

I kept my eyes closed and felt myself lift into the air. I floated to the sky, getting warmer as I drifted higher. It was like a magic trick that could stop at any moment. I could fall and not know how to land.

FIVE YEARS OLD

36

TATER LIKED TO make sure there was syrup in every square of his waffle when we had breakfast. He didn't like maple syrup, though—only strawberry flavor. I got to spend the night with him since it was the first day of summer vacation after he finished first grade. I was going to go into kindergarten at his school when it started again. I could have done kindergarten that year, but Mom said I needed more time to transition to my new kind of life.

Tater's dad was eating breakfast with us, and he let me put chocolate chips on my waffles. Tater's parents were getting divorced, so his mom wasn't there that day. I wasn't sure why they were breaking up, but Tater said she was moving to another city to live with a woman named Cypress. He said they met on the internet.

I always had strange feelings about Tater's dad, and I was starting to understand why. Because my dad hadn't been around in person, I thought most dads had jobs that were somewhere else and they would have to keep up with their kids from far away. Even though I saw real dads around, I didn't really know what they did. I once heard a kid say he had four dads. He said that some kids were jealous of all his dads. Anyway, I liked Tater's dad and he was fun to be around. I liked when he made us waffles.

Mom picked me up later that morning and we went to pick up Daddy at the hospital. He saw a doctor there, who would check the skin on his face, arms, and chest. When we were finally allowed to visit him, he looked really scary. I was a little afraid of him and sometimes couldn't breathe normal when I looked right at him. It was hard for him to talk for a while, and he had different operations to put replacement skin on. Some of it was skin from other parts of his body. I didn't know they could do that. I remembered the time I broke my arm, but they didn't have to put other skin on it. I guess it was easier to fix than a face.

The way Daddy looked was kind of like the moon at first. But then the moon itself started to look different to me— almost like it had never had a face. It became just a moon, and it was a million miles away.

As far as talking went, Daddy's mouth was healing, but he still had to go to another doctor whose job it was to teach him how to speak better.

He practiced saying words in short sentences, so the skin on his face didn't get too sore. He would tell me little things about himself. For example: He likes to read mystery books. He likes ice cream. He likes boats and the river. He wants to go to Hawaii someday. He wants to teach me how to play basketball. He likes making breakfast. And there are things he doesn't like: pears, oatmeal, raisins, cigarette smoke, and wearing a hat. But he had to wear a hat sometimes because his hair didn't look normal yet.

"Just call me Dad now," he said when he first came home. When I called him Daddy, it made him laugh too much, and it hurts to laugh, he said.

He said living with us was a lot nicer than jail. And he said we can even move to a bigger place when Mom wanted to. Home felt like a totally different thing with him there. With us.

smile. He closed his eyes as he listened, and it seemed like he was going to fall asleep right there, standing up. I want to fall asleep standing up, too, I thought.

Mom finished the story and I felt my eyes starting to close. I always thought that when you fell asleep, your eyes fell asleep first, and then the rest of your body did. Maybe that's why I could fly in some of my dreams. Maybe that's why Dad could sleep standing up.

"Hey," Mom whispered in my ear. "Look at your dad."

My eyes opened and I looked over to him, leaning against the doorway. His eyes opened too, and we looked at each other.

ACKNOWLEDGMENTS

THIS BOOK WAS such a long time in the making. Through eight years of writing, and another four years of struggles with agents and potential publishers, I finally found a publisher willing to take a chance on this story—a book I often referred to as "an impossible novel." Thank you, Patrick Barber, for your hard work, your care, and your collaborative spirit with Tony Volcano and his weird story.

I would like to thank every friend I've had since 2011. You think I'm joking, but I'm serious! Close friends, distant friends, new friends, old friends, and kind acquaintances: You are my chosen family.

Mostly, I want to give big giant hugs to: Kirk Read, Jay Ponteri. Emma Alden, Joshua James Amberson, Jeff Alessandrelli, Stacy Kirages, Felicity Fenton, Michael Heald, Justin Hocking, Mike Daily, Kate Jayroe, Kimberly King Parsons, Tia Factor, Ash Yang-Thompson, Kara Vernor, Kellette Elliott, Chrys Tobey, Bianca Flores, Jeffrey Yamaguchi, Emilly Prado, Jay Berrones, Katherine Morgan, Gary Fisketjon, Cheryl Chudyk, Stephen Kurowski, Lori Blumenthal, Cheryl Strayed, Kurt Eisenlohr, Jennifer Robin, Emme Lund, Charlie J. Stephens, Karen Russell, Caren Beilin, Miriam Toews, Rita Bullwinkel, Marti Zimlin, Lydia Kiesling, Omar El Akkad, Frayn Masters, Genevieve Hudson, Elle Nash, Chelsea Bieker, Leni Zumas,

Luca Dipierro, Carla Crujido, Michael Seidlinger, allison anne, Justin Taylor, Dena Rash Guzman, Chelsea Hodson, Leah Sottile, Santi Elijah Holley, Patrick deWitt, Shane Kowalski, Ash Iubatti, Susie Bright, Pauls Toutonghi, Claire Hopple, Nate Lippens, Jon Raymond, Emily Chenoweth, Raf Frumkin, Aaron Gilbreath, Emily Kendal Frey, Willy Vlautin, Andrew Monko, Jude Brewer, Garielle Lutz, Lidia Yuknavitch, Russ Foust, Aaron Beebe, Zachary Schomburg, Jessica Poundstone, Paulann Petersen, Alicia Jo Rabins, Nick Yandell, Monica Drake, Kurtiss Lofstrom, Cari Luna, Peter Rock, Joe O'Brien, Justin Rigamonti, Amy Harper, Joshua Mohr, Brandon Freels, Olivia Hammerman, Ryan Hall, Wendy C. Ortiz, Mark Russell, Davy Rothbart, Torea Frey, Bobby Rea, Dayvid Figler, Ellena Rosenthal, Gigi Little, Linda Watson, Jason Chan, Dianah Hughley, Laural Winter, Reuben Nisenfeld, Luke Goebel, Steve Arndt, Laura Stanfill, Melissa Amstutz, Sam Berman, and Jade Chan.

Thank you to my Powell's people, my collage comrades, and my Future Tense Books family.

Shout out to all the independent booksellers who support and hype books published by small presses.

Thanks to two things that came at just the right time, in 2019: My grant from RACC (Regional Arts & Culture Council) and Wellbutrin.

To those gone too soon: Arthur Franklin, Bryan Coffelt, André Ricciardi, and Patrick Bocarde.

For my sweet mother, Patsy (1929–2020).

To my best brother, Matt Sampsell.

To my awesome son, Zacharath.

To my partner, Katie Price. I always dreamed of a love this good. Thank you for your heart.

KEVIN SAMPSELL
PORTLAND, OREGON
FEBRUARY 2026

ABOUT THE AUTHOR

KEVIN SAMPSELL is the author of the novel *This Is Between Us* (Tin House Books) and the memoir *A Common Pornography* (Harper Perennial). He also edited the anthology *Portland Noir* (Akashic Books). His short fiction and essays have appeared in many publications and anthologies, including *Best American Essays*. A collection of his collage art and poetry, *I Made an Accident,* was published by Clash Books in 2022. Sampsell lives in Portland, Oregon, where he has run the small press Future Tense Books since 1992, and has been a bookseller and events coordinator at Powell's City of Books since 1997.

OTHER BOOKS BY KEVIN SAMPSELL

Sean the Stick
I Made an Accident: Collages and Poems
This Is Between Us
A Common Pornography
Creamy Bullets
Beautiful Blemish

Portland Noir (editor)
The Insomniac Reader (editor)

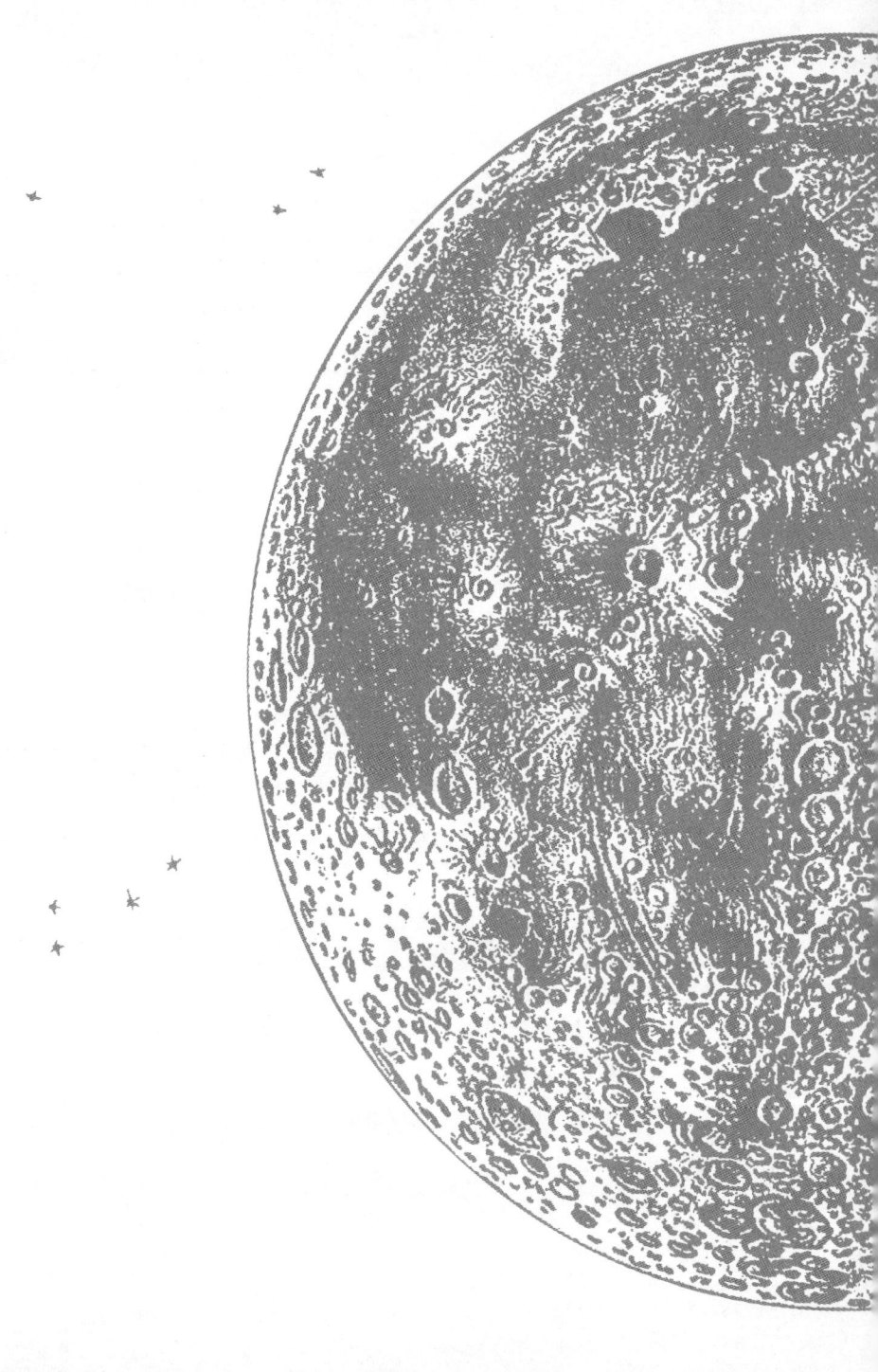